THE
Fighting Man

THE
Fighting Man

David Johnstone

METHUEN

For my mother and father

First published 1986
by Methuen Children's Books Ltd
11 New Fetter Lane, London EC4P 4EE
Copyright © 1986 David Johnstone
Printed in Great Britain

British Library Cataloguing in Publication Data

Johnstone, David, 1945–
  The fighting man.
  I. Title
  823'.914[F]   PZ7

ISBN 0-416-96960-7

Contents

Pay them back woe for woe
Give them back blow for blow
Out and make way for the bold Fenian man

PROLOGUE
Ireland 1845

The first sound was the tramp of marching feet. The old man in the ditch screwed up his ugly face and muttered to himself. Harsh it was; the feet beating their regular rhythm, a crunch of steel-shod boots on stone.

The old man straightened to watch as the platoon of soldiers swung into view, stepping out briskly.

'What is it today, my lovely boys, my brave buckos?' he cried in a high cracked voice. 'Who is it you are wanting today?'

A halt was called. There was a final smart crunch then silence. The sun glinted among the purple heather of the hilltops, a lark sang high and far away.

A young officer, dark and nervous, detached himself from the party and walked over to the ditch.

'A grand govinment,' observed the old man under his breath. 'We beg them for food and they give us soldiers. 'Tis a grand govinment!'

Constrained as he was in the ditch the old man contrived to cut a caper, to dance a sort of jig. 'Isn't it the grand govinment!'

The officer's face was pale and set. 'Stop your foolery, grandfather,' he said. 'We have come for Patrick O'Fee. This is his village.'

If you could call it a village. A collection of turf-roofed cabins huddling like sheep beneath the hills and the fat rain-bellied clouds which, even now, were massing overhead. Nothing like an English village; nothing like Monkton. 'Which is his dwelling?'

'Now then, you're asking me.' The old man had resumed his labours. He was picking dock leaves. 'Is it me should be telling you? It was Pat who took the shot at Mister Egan the land agent. I do not think so highly of Pat for what he did,' he cleared his throat and spat, repeating his ugly grin. 'For he missed his shot, bad cess to him.'

'For shame. Is that a fitting manner for one with your grey hairs to talk?'

'Is it not Egan who is driving us off our land when we have not the rent to pay him? We are starving yet he continues to drive and harry us as if we were animals.' The old man turned his dark ringed eyes on the young officer; they were burning with a light sometimes seen in madmen. 'If he was lying stiff and cold there in the ditch before me, I should spit on him.' He suited the action to the words and continued picking.

'There is a rule of law which should be obeyed.' There was a barely perceptible falter in the officer's voice which grew hoarser. 'Tell us where Patrick O'Fee lives or you shall show us at the point of a bayonet.'

'I almost have enough, your honour.' The old man displayed his bunch of leaves. 'We sprinkle these with a little vinegar – I have a wife and three hungry grandchilder – vinegar for relish, you understand. It makes the grand dinner for us. What is it your honour will be eating at the barracks in Castletown, beef would it be? And will you be having it roast or boiled? I'll tell the childer what the fine soldiers get to eat.'

'Excuse me, sir.' The corporal, a short fair-haired man, grown somewhat pink during this exchange, marched smartly over, knocked the leaves from the old man's hands and ground them underfoot. 'Now then, you old sinner, the next thing I kick shall be your head. Will you answer the officer's question or won't you?'

'Ach well,' the old man's face broke into its grin, 'sure, it was only me little bit of fun. There's nobody enjoys to see the soldiers march more than myself. That's Pat's cabin over yonder – but take a warning, sir. He's in a desperate way is Pat, he fears no man, not all the soldiers in the country. Rule Britannia!' This last was shouted after them in his cracked old voice, 'It's a grand govinment! God's curse on all of you and your black hearts!' He carried on muttering and turned away frowning, as if he had been distracted from the serious business of life.

The soldiers organised themselves into two groups. The first

10

remained by the low stone wall with fixed bayonets; the second, under the command of the young officer, made their way through a green and boggy meadow until they had encircled the cabin. There was the heavy sweet smell of decay on the air.

At a given command two of the troopers began beating a heavy tattoo on the door with the stocks of their rifles.

In the interval that followed the pounding one of them observed, 'I don't reckon the door is bolted, sir.'

It wasn't. The officer and the corporal were the first to enter and stood blinking in the gloom. The smell was nigh on unbearable, heavy and fetid.

'There!' Something stirred and both men sprang back, arms at the ready. A soft scuttling movement and a rat ran over the corporal's boots and out into the open field.

'Easy,' the corporal pointed with his pistol. 'Over there.'

As their eyes grew used to the light they could see a pile of straw and a blanket partly covering something. There was nothing in the bare bothy worth remark; a dead fire, a cooking pot, long dead, long empty, lying on its side.

'Take it easy, Mister Condent,' said the corporal, laying his hand on the young lieutenant's arm. 'This ain't going to be pretty, sir.'

They both looked down as the corporal flicked the blanket back.

'That's the one, sir.' Patrick O'Fee stared at them from open, blank eyes, his cheeks were sunken and full of shadow, his lips drawn back against two great yellow teeth, like a horse's. 'He shan't be bothering no one else. Small wonder he missed his shot, he wouldn't have had the strength to lift more'n a pea shooter. He's been dead some time – '

'The rat?' whispered the lieutenant, horror struck.

'Got to him afore we did.' The corporal took hold of Patrick O'Fee's arm as if it was a piece of dead wood. The hand was still gripped around the ancient fowling piece, the very weapon used to shoot at the land agent, though which was the colder, the hand or the gun, was hard to say. 'I've a daughter of twelve month whose arms are plumper than this,' the corporal added.

The young officer shuddered convulsively and turned away.

11

Kicking aside the miserable door of the hovel, he strode out into the field and stood alone, drawing great shuddering gulps of air.

The hills, turning darker as the clouds gathered, frowned down on the single red speck; the soldier. Everywhere, like a mist, hung the sweet smell of decay and rottenness.

'Beggin' your pardon, Lieutenant Condent, sir.' The corporal, honest blue eyes clouded over, was at his elbow.

'A fine soldier I make, eh corporal?' Lieutenant Condent sat down abruptly on a rough boulder.

The corporal looked down at him. If he'd married at eighteen – which he nearly did, God help him – he'd have a lad this boy's age.

'I think so, sir. You're a bold 'un and you have the devil in you sir, beggin' your pardon once more. But you come from an Irish family, sir. This can't be easy.'

The Lieutenant studied his boots where the wet had soaked into them. 'Yes. Though I was never in Ireland before this year. I grew up in Monkton, Somerset. My mother lives there. Our Irish lands were sold up long ago but you are right, part of me is Irish and this is the most loathsome work man was ever put to.'

It had grown cooler, soon it would rain but the young lieutenant made no attempt to move.

'The poor people. Even the men grumble at some of the things we ask them to do. The smell, I suppose, is the potatoes?'

'Aye, over this way. Come and look.'

Twenty yards behind the bothy a pit had been dug. Covered in straw and earth, it was where the potatoes were stored. When they were clamped they had been white and spotless; a day later they had begun to decay. Now they were a putrid black mass where hordes of flies gorged themselves. Across the country the whole crop had been struck by this mysterious blight. Now the people were starving; potatoes were their staple food.

'A good year for flies,' observed the corporal, without a trace of humour.

The two soldiers turned away and walked slowly back to where their men were waiting.

'Tell them to stand easy,' said Lieutenant Condent. 'Do we dispose of the body?'

'Perhaps he has some sort of family,' said the corporal, with a shrug. 'Somewhere. Though it looks as though they have all gone along before him. No doubt the priest will wish to cant over him.'

The young officer was heart sick. The poor people; *his* people. Those who were starving could not pay their rent; if they did not pay their rent they were evicted. Though the troopers hated the work and grumbled at it they did it efficiently, without mercy.

A soft rain had begun to fall. Oh, Finn Mac Cool . . .

'What's that, sir?' The corporal had been whistling tunelessly.

Lieutenant Condent flushed, suddenly embarrassed, 'Have you never heard of the great Irish hero, Finn Mac Cool?'

'Can't say as I have, sir. Some sort of Robin Hood was he?'

'I had an Irish nurse when I was a boy.' The Lieutenant studied the dwelling, where the sag of skin and bones known as Patrick O'Fee lay. 'She told me stories of Finn every night before I slept. Finn Mac Cool who could course a deer on his bare feet, who had the thumb of knowledge, who defended Ireland against all her enemies, natural or supernatural.'

'He sounds quite a lad, sir. They could do with someone like him now.'

Lieutenant Condent looked at the cabins huddled on the hillside. 'It all happened here. Here, where our soldiers tear the roofs from their houses, where people are dogged and driven and die in the ditches in their scores. Where is he now, I wonder?'

The corporal looked at his lieutenant sombrely. He was not an imaginative man; stories were for children. On the wind was the scent of putrid potatoes and the rain hissed down all around them. But the rain streaked their cheeks like tears; as if someone should have been crying.

'They sure as God need something, sir,' he said. 'Somebody ought to do something.'

CHAPTER ONE
The Bold Fenian Men

Manchester 1867: a grey afternoon and melancholy; squalls of rain bursting on the exposed figures clinging to the outside of the prison van.

'A lonely road,' observed the driver to his mate.

And a long one, he might have added; and dangerous, with these two damned Fenians aboard.

The policemen behind, like so many grim-faced postilions, bent their tall hats against the weather, as if praying for a safe passage.

Blasted Fenians. Somebody could have been killed this afternoon outside the courtroom. Constable Hardwick could have been snuffed out; Hardwick put out like a candle wick. Goodnight Hardwick and five bawling orphans in the morning. Fenians –

'What are these plaguey Fenians, any road?' demanded the driver, whose name was Dick.

'Irish.' His mate, by name Jack, was a man with no neck at all. He always said it had been took up into his head on account of all the scrunching up he was required to do against the weather. Certainly his head was very fat. 'Don't this rain go down your collar, though?'

'I know they're Irish,' Dick spat genteelly into the street below. 'Mother Murphy who does my laundry is Irish. I have nowt against her for that. What do these lads complain of?'

'These boys,' responded his mate, giving the roof of the van a smart rap with his whip by way of emphasis, 'want Ireland to be ruled by the likes of them'

'What, no Her Majesty?'

'Kick out the English, Her Majesty and all the rest of 'em.'

'God bless us,' said Dick. 'Revolutionaries.'

'Ireland for the Irish.'

Dick shook his head, 'Welcome, I'd say.'

'And if they don't get it they'll blow us all up in our beds. There's so many on 'em, see. Mother Murphy and the rest of 'em, they're everywhere. That's where we made our big mistake, letting them all in. I daresay they dig the roads and canals well enough, but even then they're taking the bread from honest English mouths. And they're all ready to blow us up when the head Fenians say so. Stop at nothing – that's why yer lads were hanging about the courtroom this afternoon. I was reading it all in this morning's *Gazette*. These two, Colonel Kelly and Captain Deasy they call 'em, are big nobs and the Fenians would do anything to have them back.'

Two men had been spotted loitering outside the courtroom where the two Fenian leaders were being remanded; watching as the leaders were herded into the prison van with a number of common criminals. The valiant Constable Hardwick had challenged them; and a knife, glinting like water in the grey afternoon, nearly ended his life.

'Did you hear the way Kelly and Deasy talk?' demanded Dick's mate. 'American. A lot of these Fenians served in the American Civil War – not afraid of guns or gunpowder, and know how to use 'em.'

'American or not,' grunted Dick, 't'would be a set of madmen to try owt wi' this set of bluebottles buzzing around.' He jerked his head at the unusual number of policemen clutching to the back of the van. 'Giddup, Edgar – tha'll meet thisself coming back if tha' doesn't hurry.'

They were creaking and lurching along at a snail's pace; a funeral van, in mourning for the lost liberty of those it carried through the dismal streets. The policemen's helmets bobbing like so many plumes as the rain bounced and skittered along the roof.

'Pull on, Edgar. Pull on, John.'

Thus addressed, the two horses plunged their heads, but the van came on with no increase of pace. They were reaching the viaduct which took the London and North Western railway across the road. There were houses to the left, to the right sooty fields with nothing in them but nettles and rubbish.

15

Another rush of rain before the arch flung its gloomy arm over them and they were blinking at the change. White faces stared mutely up at them like mourners watching the cortège pass by. Then out in the light once more, to find their way barred by a group of men standing sullenly in the road. They appeared to be labourers and mechanicals for the most part, with here and there, on the fringes, a dark suit. All of them were armed, mainly with firearms, the rest with pickaxes.

Dick turned to his mate in dismay but what he said was destroyed by the terrific volley of gunfire that greeted their emergence into the light. Most of the shots were aimed high but all the policemen dropped at once to the ground; one of them was hit and he lay groaning, clutching at his thigh with bloodied hands. The horses, badly frighted, began to scream and plunge. Dick, discovering that he was not dead, was barely able to bring them under control. He thought about giving them their heads, but while the notion formed, a dark bearded man ran over and clapping a revolver to Edgar's temple, shot him dead.

Dick stared down stupidly.

'You've shot the horse.'

The man, whose beard was peculiar by being streaked with grey both sides, ignored the dying agony of the dumb animal and reared the revolver so it pointed to those in the driving seat. It was hard to say which looked the more deadly; the barrel of the gun or the dark eyes behind it.

Even at the extremity of fear Dick could not restrain a look of disgust.

'There weren't no call to kill Edgar.'

'Get down,' the dark man spoke without heat, he indicated a spot at the verge of the road. 'We are Fenians. We have come to relieve you of your prisoners.'

At another signal from him a group of men, armed with picks and bayonets, was brought up. They clambered on to the roof of the van and set about it with a series of ringing blows which filled the street with a hollow booming. Those Fenians with firearms stood in a rough half circle, spreading themselves wide about the vehicle, keeping the police and the growing number of bystanders at bay; loosing off an occasional shot from time to time by way of a frightener. The police watched stolidly, tending their wounded comrade, his groans inaudible beneath the blows of the axes. Then another shot would be fired, sending the bystanders ducking and scrambling for safety.

It was plain the bearded man was the Fenian leader. He kept up a restless movement, conferring with the men on the roof, restraining the more impulsive of his gunmen, consulting his watch, glancing up and down the road quickly. Everyone deferred to him, addressing him more than once as 'Captain'. He had put his gun away but his steps were dogged by a small red haired man with a quick nervous face who fairly bristled with weapons. This lieutenant brandished a revolver in one hand, while another was stuffed into the top of his trousers; over one shoulder was slung a full belt of cartridges, over the other a rifle. This was Desmond.

'Now then, gentlemen,' said the captain, returning to the spot where Dick and Jack were squatting and resting his foot upon a stone which bore the information that Salford was some miles distant, 'the boys up top compliment you on the construction of your van – opening it up is taking longer than we anticipated. The question I put to you is this – who has the key?'

Dick and his mate exchanged glances.

'I have some hotheads with me,' remarked the captain, noting the expression that had passed between the two. 'They would like nothing better than to ventilate one or two of the boys in blue there – '

'And why not?' interrupted Desmond with ferocity, snapping at the Captain's heels.

'Why not, Desmond?' The captain turned calmly to his lieutenant. 'We have a simple job to do. We want no extra fuss. Now then, who has the key?'

Desmond made an angry gesture but it was plain the captain had him leashed. Dick set his mouth firmly and folded his arms. He was still grieved over the death of Edgar.

'Time does not allow patience,' said the Captain mildly. The revolver had reappeared in his hand.

'It's Charlie you want . . . Charlie Brett,' stammered Jack.

17

'And which one is Charlie Brett?' asked the Captain, speaking carefully, as if addressing a child.

Dick burst out with a rough laugh. 'None of 'em,' he said and looked away again. The men on the roof had stopped banging and were following the conversation with interest.

The captain's brows drew together; his thumb cocked the revolver.

'No – no!' the driver's mate burst in hoarsely, setting his head even deeper into his shoulders, as if avoiding a blow. 'It's the truth. May God strike me blind if I lie. Charlie isn't there, he's inside the van. He locked himself in after the trouble outside the courtroom.'

The captain turned to Desmond. 'Ask Charlie to unlock the door. If he won't, shoot the lock off.' Another shot had gone off followed by a shriek of pain. He turned on his heel and hurried away.

The lock on the prison van was an imposing block of metal. Like a paving slab, Desmond thought to himself, what if there were bolts on the other side? The door held a grating; he could hear a man and a woman, or was it two women, talking.

Desmond licked his lips and put his face to the grating. 'Charlie Brett?'

More whispering.

'Charlie Brett, we know you're in there.'

'Aye, I'm in here.' It was a flat voice; like a wall.

Desmond cocked his revolver, the way he had seen the Captain do it.

'Open the door, Charlie Brett.'

The whispering died.

'You know who we want – Kelly and Deasy. We want them now. Let them out and we won't hurt you.'

Silence.

Desmond was a small man; he had the quick temper of many small men. He wiped his sweating palms on his jacket.

'Open the doors and let your prisoners out!' he cried; his mouth was dry. What he wouldn't do for a good cup of tea to wet his whistle.

'I dursn't,' said the voice gloomily. There loomed towards him a sad face with drooping moustaches. A man who knew his duty and would do it.

'Look.' Desmond swallowed, he was on fire. If only he had something to drink. The gun was hot in his hand. 'We're going to kill you. Give us the keys.'

There was a lengthy pause while Charlie Brett weighed this on the scales of his dutiful mind before pronouncing his doom.

'I can't.'

There was an enormous flash and bang. Before the smoke had begun to clear the women within were screaming in hysterics.

Desmond lowered his revolver and gazed in with wide eyes; Charlie Brett was gone.

He was violently wrenched away from the grating and shoved to one side.

'God help us, Allan,' Desmond said, licking his lips, 'I was shooting at the lock.'

The captain put his face to the grating. 'How bad is it?' he demanded.

The women answered in a shrieking chorus –

'Mother of Mercy, he's dead – '

'Shot through the very bowels. Save us all – '

'Well,' said the captain loudly. 'I have a madman out here who's wanting to let off his gun once more. You'd like to stop that now, wouldn't you?'

He spoke with the same kindness he had shown to Dick and his mate, 'Charlie will have the keys in his pocket or on his belt – all you have to do is to get them out.'

'God have mercy,' the other woman could be heard urging her companion to get the keys out of Charlie's pocket. The way they spoke of poor Charlie it was plain they were well acquainted with him. The key was found without further difficulty and the heavy door unlocked. The captain entered, avoiding Charlie's body, taking the bunch of keys from the older woman whose garish face and jaunty hat were sadly at odds with her terrified expression.

The interior of the prison van consisted of a series of locked stalls on either side of a main passage. Evidently Charlie had not considered it necessary to lock the women up.

'Where's Pat Kelly?' called the captain.

'In here,' came the reply.

This set up a chorus of pleas from the other prisoners. The bearded captain ignored them as he tried the first two keys on the ring. Desmond did not come in but stayed gazing down on Charlie Brett. The women pressed away from the long revolver now held loosely over his arm.

'Yer a fine big lad,' muttered the younger woman scornfully.

The third key opened the stall and Colonel Kelly stepped out.

'Well, Allan,' he said, 'this is well done. You will find Mr Deasy yonder.' He was a man not much above middle height. His hair, like the captain's, was cropped short and he too sported a full beard. He was dressed in a respectable grey coat and trousers; he looked like no one's idea of a revolutionary.

'We have been too long at this,' the captain said as he opened the door of the second stall. 'They will be bringing up the soldiers.'

'We have faced worse together,' observed Kelly, glancing carelessly at the body of Charlie Brett and at Desmond who still guarded the doorway.

'This is the last time, for all that,' replied the captain. 'This is my last blow for the Brotherhood. There are others outside who will guide you to safety. Once you leave this van our ways will part.'

'So that's it?'

'That's the way of it. I'm for France.' He too, looked down at the body on the floor. 'I've had my bellyful of the killing trade. Desmond is your man now. I will do all I can for the movement from abroad.'

Deasy had joined Kelly. He touched his leader's elbow.

'Well,' Kelly extended his hand. 'This is not the time to argue the point. You have proved you are a true-hearted Irishman on a score of occasions, Allan Condent. I was never one of those to mistrust your service in the British Army, we have seen too much together for that. I will not forget this day's work.'

They shook hands. Deasy had already left the van.

'Kelly – I will die for you!' cried Desmond fervently.

Kelly looked back at the dark captain. 'Allan,' he said, 'there is a saying about omelettes and eggs, you know.'

Then he was gone.

The captain looked at Charlie Brett; he took off his hat and a spasm crossed his face. He was remembering Dick's expression after he shot his horse.

Then he, too, stepped out into the rainy afternoon.

CHAPTER TWO
Monkton Mill

Through the window Allan Condent could see the boy reading. His hair golden in the lamplight, swept aside by the hand which cradled his face. Allan closed one eye, like a man looking along a rifle barrel, and sighted him through a pane of the glass: a boy to be proud of.

The lighted window threw its pattern of squares and diamonds across the black water of the river to where he sheltered beneath the poplars on the opposite bank. Rain, blowing slowly along the valley, pattered among the leaves. The trees bent their heads and whispered to one another. He counted them as they stood in their row along the river bank and sighed. The breath was snatched from his lips by the wind and tossed among the rain, the river, the whispering trees. It was all as he remembered.

Finn Hagan was alone that night. The mill and all its outbuildings lay entirely in his care. Not that he minded; it was the mill dog, Sam, who paced the kitchen uneasily. The kitchen was filled with blue smoke from the fire where the wind boomed in the chimney like guns. Finn merely coughed, rubbed his eyes and read on.

Several times Sam stood by the door with his ears pricked, turning to his master with a meaningful look. Finn ignored him until he began to growl.

'The wind,' mumbled the boy without lifting his head. 'Do leave off, there's a good dog, or I'll put you out in the rain.'

Sam barked in contradiction. At the same time came a soft knocking.

Finn picked up the lamp at once. The mill, tucked as it was in the shelter of Castle Hill, was on the way to nowhere. It was too late for trade and what neighbours they had walked in unannounced.

'Who is it there?' demanded Finn, keeping one hand on Sam and feeling a growl thrill in his throat. 'Speak up.'

'A friend,' came the quiet reply.

The door swung open to reveal a man, whose broad brimmed hat dripped rain; whose coat, slick with it, made pools on the kitchen floor. A bearded, sunburnt man, whose beard was touched either side with grey, like a badger; whose steady brown eyes bent down into his. His boots were square-toed and sounded harsh on the stone flags of the kitchen floor. Behind him, over the river and across the fields, an owl screeched.

'No further, Mister Friend.' Finn thrust the lamp towards the stranger while Sam growled deep in his belly.

His visitor paused. 'You would not refuse me a warm at your fire? I am somewhat damp.'

With perfect indifference he advanced into the room, throwing open his coat. He put a foot on the bars of the fire and watched it steam and hiss.

'I'll warrant the shotgun on the wall there is not loaded,' he observed, changing the foot he held up to the fire. 'Besides, your father is not so rich in friends that he can afford to have his son shoot one of them.' He laughed softly, 'Mister Friend,' he said to himself.

Finn was nonplussed. It was true he had contemplated snatching down the gun and threatening the stranger with it. Faced with such composure it was difficult for a thirteen-year-old boy to decide what to do. He could set the dog on him but there was something in the negligent way in which the man held himself that hinted that Sam would not have it all his own way. Besides, Sam was too old and fat now to be really fierce.

'You have business with my father?' he said, as coolly as he could. 'He will be home shortly.'

'I knew him before you were born.' Satisfied that his feet were more comfortable the stranger took off his hat and looked about him with a bright eye. 'We were comrades once in the old country. I know all about you, Finn Hagan – how you have lived in this England all your life and at this mill for the past three months. But for all that, you are a pure bred Irishman. Like myself. Never forget that. So let us sit down together.'

'You know a lot about me,' said Finn, closing out the wind and the rain, 'but nothing I didn't know already,' he added beneath his breath.

By the firelight the stranger's dark face was full of shadow. His black hair was cropped close to his head; by way of a contrast his beard was thick and curly, streaked with grey.

'You will know me again, I'm thinking,' the stranger remarked.

'It was your name I did not catch,' said Finn.

His visitor showed his teeth and laughed quietly. 'Call me Mister Friend for the now. Do you know, wet as I am on the outside, a glass of home brew would not go amiss.'

Finn ground his teeth; but as hospitality was an iron rule in his father's house he complied without comment.

He returned after drawing the beer to discover his visitor in the best chair, having donned a pair of gold-rimmed spectacles which lent him an oddly scholarly air. He was reading Finn's book.

'*Old Mortality*,' said the stranger. 'I wondered what it was that drew your nose so close. So that is the sort of tale you admire – you see yourself helping a fugitive evade justice?'

'Is that what you came for?' asked Finn, without expression.

'Damn your impudence,' replied the stranger and chuckled, though the laugh did not come as easily as it might have. 'Though stranger things have been asked of young people before now.' He changed the subject. 'This is a Scotch tale, have you nothing Irish to read?'

'I have not,' said Finn shortly.

'I forgot,' the stranger put a finger to his lips. 'Do you know I think I know as much about you as you do yourself. It is your mother; she will let you hear no Irish stories, nor will she talk of the bitter past. She wants to do away with old enmities – to forgive the English. So you will not have heard of the person whose name you bear – Finn Mac Cool?'

'Mother says . . .' Finn's hand strayed towards his hair; his name was something to do with that –

'Finn means fair? But what about Finn Mac Cool who ran down a deer on his bare feet. The greatest warrior Erin has ever known? When I was well below your age a woman named Annie

24

crooned those stories into my ear in the half dark while I waited for sleep. They have been the stuff of my dreams ever since – ' He touched his fingers to his forehead, 'They are with me yet, so that when I walk in . . . certain places, I see Finn and his warriors run before me. Finn MacCool who could see the future. God help us.'

'You know an uncommon lot about our family.'

'There is a communication between us. Your father gives me all your news.' The stranger settled back in his chair. 'So, how do you find life in Monkton?'

'Well enough,' replied Finn, relaxing a little. 'Father has dragged us from pillar to post, from place to place, all my life. I like it well enough to want to stay.'

The stranger's eye looked brighter than ever.

'But the people hereabouts . . . Father says they hate our guts.'

'Your father was brought in over the heads of some local men,' said the stranger. 'Though they need a mill they do not feel they need to love the miller. It warms me to hear you say it, that you like it well here. I have seen many places in my life, from the lakes of Killarney to the banks of the Missouri, yet the memory of this spot has travelled with me. Tell me, how many poplars stand on the opposite bank yonder?'

'Seven,' replied Finn, promptly.

'Seven,' said the stranger. 'Just so. It is seven.'

He allowed the conversation to flag at this point. Finn pretended to read but the spell was broken; his mind set dancing to a different tune. His eye kept straying to the visitor who, much tired, had begun to drowse by the fire. His hands were thrust deep into the sleeves of his coat which steamed as it dried. He was bent forward, in an attitude which put Finn in mind of the monks of olden times. No, he thought suddenly, with a quick intuition that sent a shiver through him, more like a soldier snatching a rest during a lull in the battle.

It was late. Thinking turned to dreaming and as he drowsed Finn imagined that the stranger was watching him with eyes that smouldered and flared like the coals of the fire. Proud the eyes were, and warm; so that he felt safe, like a small child once more.

Sam barked. The stranger's hand was stretched out to his face.

He awoke startled, sharp fright in his heart, only to see the visitor bent in the same posture, hands tucked away in the sleeves of his coat.

Dermot Hagan was in the room, shaking the rain from himself like a great shaggy wet dog.

'Give us a glim here, Finn, the night is black.'

'As black as original sin,' said the man by the fire.

Dermot spilled the basket he was carrying, dropping a score of eggs on the stone floor. A cloud of mingled emotions crossed his face as a shadow crosses the sun.

'The name of God,' he said. 'Allan, is that you?'

He stooped forward for a better view, spurning the eggs with heedless feet. 'Allan.'

The stranger laughed, 'You know me then – or was it the old password?'

'I know you,' Dermot Hagan's great chest shuddered. 'You are welcome.'

They made a contrast as they embraced; the tall figure of the stranger stooping to the burly miller. Finn was astonished to see tears in his father's eyes.

'Captain, my heart is weary for you,' muttered Dermot. 'You were not recognised?'

'It is almost twenty years now, Dermot. Besides, I was set down in Porlock and I walked across the moor. It was dark when I came to the village.'

'It was your home once.'

'A lifetime ago. All is well?'

'All is well.' Dermot indicated the mill with a comprehensive sweep of his arm. 'You have made a man of substance of me.'

'You were always that,' returned Allan with a wry smile. 'And I fancy that voice of yours rattles the windows when the mill wheel is grinding. You were always excited by machinery. But here is Mary, does she know me too?'

Finn's mother, hooded, the rain drops spangling in the light, was looking not at the stranger but at her son. She too, seemed moved.

'You are changed,' she said finally.

'God Almighty, I forgot,' interrupted Dermot, laying a hand on the stranger's arm. 'We are to have a child soon. It will be a boy, born in time for Christmas. I prayed this morning it would be a boy and will have a Mass said to make double sure.'

'A brother for Finn,' said Mary Hagan.

''Tis a grand thing to have a family,' said the stranger, looking at her.

'Finn does a man's work these days.' Dermot laid a heavy hand on the boy's shoulder. 'But he should not be asked to watch so far into the night. He is white with want of sleep.'

'I am not a child,' said Finn, shifting his shoulder.

Dermot raised a shaggy eyebrow, 'Do you say so?'

He bent and threw some wood on to the fire. 'Mary, my belly is clapping its chops. I have not ate since tea-time and the captain here will want feeding.'

He turned to Finn, 'For all that, my mannie, you will be at the school when it reopens. Begob, they are a lawless lot in this village. The Inspectors came and closed down the school in March. It was cold you see, so some of the boys chopped up their forms to fuel the stove. They say the master stood by and pulled at his own hair while they did it. Now Lady Condent has hired a new man who knows his trade – they say he comes down directly. I do not envy him his job.'

'Lady Condent – ' the stranger put in eagerly. 'You have spoken with her?'

Dermot shook his head, 'I will tell you no lie, I have yet to put my eyes to her. She sees no one but this chaplain she took up with in London. They are opening a home for ragged children up there. As if there were not enough children on her own estate with their backsides hanging out.'

'But the steward, Vellew, he treats you well?'

Dermot shrugged and shook his tousle of fair curly hair. 'He's such a timid wee man. He sits on that little horse of his and whispers his messages. But he did arrange for the boy here to take tea with her ladyship.'

The stranger's eyes kindled once more but Dermot shook his head. 'A disaster. She was high and mighty and when Pinecoffin – that is the chaplain's name – wheedled out of Finn that he went to Mass on Sundays that was the end of his chances.'

Finn frowned. He had been told that it was her Ladyship's custom to invite the mill children to tea once. His chances of what?

'Tell the captain what the old bible-basher said to you, Finn.'

'A good deal I don't remember,' replied Finn. 'He ranted at me as if I was a congregation all to myself. Stuff about the Whore of Babylon and the Pope – ' He blushed and glanced quickly at his mother who was cleaning the mess Dermot had made with the eggs. 'Before that they were speaking about their cause and how the children in London pray every night for Lady Condent. There was something about a dream too – the chaplain takes a drug for his toothache which gives him dreams about a golden city – '

'Did you ever hear such stuff?' grumbled Dermot.

'He's always outside the golden city and he can't get in.'

They had stopped listening. Finn remembered what an ordeal he'd been through; the stiff new collar, new boots that creaked coarsely along the long corridor, the amusement of the maid. Lady Condent herself, wispy grey hair and a face like an eagle's. Shoes down at heel and solid silver buckles.

'Vellew will keep trying,' said Allan Condent, at length. 'We have to do what we can.'

There was a funny thing. We have to do what we can for him, for Finn. That was the implication. They were all looking at him and he ducked his head.

His mother began to fry thick slices of ham in an iron skillet. The meat hissed in the pan and filled the kitchen with the scent of morning.

'Manchester,' Finn heard his father mutter. 'Devil a bit, I heard just such a tale from a tinker. So Kelly and Deasy run free?'

'Finn,' said his mother quietly, 'you must go to bed. Say good-night and go to bed.'

Finn listened to the voices from below. His father's was like the rumble of the mill wheel. There was one thing he hadn't said; he wouldn't know how to say it. When the chaplain had described the waifs and strays praying for Lady Condent her eyes had filled with tears. Pinecoffin had looked sharply at her, aware of the effect he was creating. Finn had felt sorry for her. That was what he couldn't say. He had felt sorry for her.

Now there came the lighter tone of the stranger's voice. Once only his father had called him Allan. Allan who?

Manchester. Kelly and Deasy. He turned these words over before he slept but could make nothing of them.

When he awoke the house was quiet. The storm had blown itself out and the room was filled with moonlight. His hands and arms looked like fish in ghostly depths.

Allan. The captain. Manchester. Kelly and Deasy. Like fish themselves the words stirred in the darkness. Without pausing Finn slipped out of bed and stood listening. They must all be asleep. Across the passage he could hear the heavy snore and muttering sigh of his father, noisy even in sleep.

Barelegged, wearing only his shirt, he crept down the stairs, touching the wall to guide himself.

The stranger was still at the table. Finn came into the room a few paces. His head was pillowed in his arms and the moon touched his dark features, lending them in repose a gentleness he had not noticed earlier.

Lying on the table, within easy reach of his sleeping hand, was a long black revolver.

CHAPTER THREE
George Dando

Black as original sin; the moon gleaming on the mother of pearl handle as it lay within reach of the outspread fingers. Then the captain had stirred a little and Finn softly closed the door on him.

When he awoke again it was broad daylight. Outside, Dermot and his journeyman, Marcus Everett, were loading flour watched by pale little Mr Vellew, Lady Condent's steward, from his grey cob. Mr Vellew took a pinch of snuff and blew his nose on a red spotted handkerchief. Dermot and Marcus whistled cheerfully and ignored him. On the hill someone was sawing logs where they had felled an elm the day before.

On the table, where the captain's head had lain, was heaped a pile of mushrooms.

'He picked them for you before he went away,' his mother clacked about the kitchen in pattens, the stone floor not yet dry from her attentions, 'to thank you for your hospitality of last night, he said. I'll cook them for your breakfast. You must tell no one he came here.'

As he put the mushroom down she picked one up. Their hands touched and she held it there for a moment.

'Who would I tell?' he asked, slowly withdrawing his hand.

'Cissie,' she replied, and began to chop off the dark earthy roots. 'You two are so very thick together these days.'

'I dreamt he was going to choke me last night,' said Finn, 'when we were sitting together. What was his name?'

She scooped up the mushrooms in her old blue apron and carried them over to wash.

'Father called him Allan.'

She plunged the mushrooms into a bowl of cold water and

watched them bobbing there, the water flecked with particles of peaty earth.

"And Captain. Captain Allan," he said distinctly. 'Why is it such a big secret?'

'There has been fighting over in Ireland this year,' she said eventually. 'And now . . . well, you will hear soon enough. The Fenians have been shooting in the streets of Manchester.'

'He is a Fenian then?' he said in a whisper. 'He did not sound too Irish to me.'

His words seemed to frighten her. She turned and he saw her mouth was set. 'We will not speak about him any more.'

'Where has he gone?'

'Far away. To France. No more.' Once she was in this mood he knew it was no use; she would not budge. Ireland and her troubles were seldom mentioned in their house. He sighed and waited for his breakfast.

It was Friday. After breakfast she gave him some money and sent him for fish. At the corner, where the mill lane joined the high road, he found his friend Cissie poking a frog with a piece of straw. When she saw Finn she pouched the frog in her apron and fell into step.

'Grammer bin telling me this story,' she announced.

Cissie lived alone with her grannie. A wise woman, much in demand at childbirth or to prescribe some home-made remedy for the screwmaticks, the infloration and the mange. Or even to provide a reliable love potion. She had stuffed Cissie's head with sayings, charms and much good sense. Cissie herself was a wild dark creature who smelled of woodsmoke and secret herbs. Of all the village she was the one who loved Finn the best; she looked up at him with her black eyes wide open.

'So they knocked on the door. And when the old wife come to open it she was heaving like a dray horse – as if she'd been running herself – terr..le short in her breathings she was.'

Witches, nocturnal goings on of a supernatural nature, stories of violent death, formed the staple of Cissie's inner life. If there were bogeymen in the story she wanted to hear it. Just now she was relaying, as gospel, how three sportsmen had chased a hare

31

through a cottage garden and watched as the animal leapt through an open window –

'They knocked on the door and the old woman were short in her breathings. Finn Hagan are you listening to me?'

'I am not,' replied Finn. He had wished to be alone to think on last night; of the gun in the kitchen; shooting in the streets of Manchester. 'Why was she so out of breath?'

Cissie's brown face screwed up like a walnut.

'I expect she was having a nod before the fire and she woke up sudden,' went on Finn, 'that's why she was so out of breath.' Normally he would have been interested in this tale; now it seemed only childish.

'Sometimes you can be very ignorant, Finn Hagan,' replied Cissie warmly.

'Or asthma,' suggested Finn mischievously.

'Asthma! That's just like your ignorance, you great sheep's head. *She was the hare.*' Cissie's temper was on a short fuse; she could not bear to be teased.

'Or the brown titus. She should have asked Grannie for a potion.'

Cissie shrieked with frustration and aimed a blow at him. She could fight as well as any boy. Finn ducked and backed off laughing despite himself.

'Lay on Macduff!' A low chuckle seemed to come from the very ground, 'Damned to him that first cries enough!'

Half hidden in the ditch, helping himself to blackberries, was a long man in a low crowned hat. He offered himself more fruit and as he twitched his moustache they had a glimpse of a yellow tooth.

'What's this, my dears,' he cried as they scrambled away from him, 'You ain't cancelling the contest? You ain't going to scratch?'

He emerged from the ditch; he was wearing a close fitting grey coat and black gloves. 'Don't let me put you off – George Dando the name, how de do – a shilling to the first one who draws blood. A shilling is a lot of money – ha!' From the air, like a conjuror, he produced the silver coin; in one movement he flicked it, snatched it and displayed it.

32

Cissie screamed and retreated. Finn was not so quick; Dando grabbed him and favoured him with a glint of the tooth.

'Let me go, will you,' demanded Finn, struggling, 'let me go – '

'A lad of spirit,' said Dando, enfolding him in a horrible embrace. 'A proper blister. If money fails we must see what love will do. Do you love me, coz?'

Finn twisted his head away from the stink of his breath.

'Will you not buss me, m'boy?' enquired Dando, grinning evilly, making a kissing movement with his lips.

Finn, crimson with disgust, struggled and kicked. The second stranger he had encountered in as many days held him close and guffawed.

'I am facetious, my proud young sir, there ain't a scrap of seriousness in my entire body. Not a particle, shred nor atom. I'd rather kiss my horse's backside.'

Half hidden by the curve of the road his mount munched contentedly, trailing its reins.

From behind Finn's lapel he drew the shilling and proferred it in his fingers. His voice dropped, 'Have you seen my friend?'

'Your friend, sir?'

'My friend, sir. A singular gent who talks like a Yankee and wears square-toed Yankee boots. A bearded friend, dear to my heart, seen hereabouts yestere'en.'

For an instant Finn almost blurted out the truth; in time his mother's warning came to him.

He hesitated. There was a degree of acuteness in the glinting eyes of Dando. His voice too, had lost its playfulness and acquired a more menacing edge.

'I may have . . .'

'Say on, coz. I am bereft and would have him restored to me.'

'You are holding me tightly, sir. My arm is hurting – '

Dando relaxed slightly. In a flash Finn wriggled free. He had taken only a couple of paces before Dando hooked the legs from under him, sending him sprawling.

'A proper blister,' he remarked coolly. 'A veritable sprig of defiance. Was thinking of cutting off was 'ee, dear?'

Finn rubbed his shins tenderly, getting his breath.

'There was tinkers here t'other day,' he confessed, remembering Dermot's remark of the previous evening. 'One of 'em had a beard.'

Dando revealed the yellow tooth in an unpleasant sneer, 'Tinkers come even lower down the social scale than strolling actors – I trod the boards myself and know as much. No, young sir. My friend, for all his Yankee ways, is a gentleman.'

'I have seen no strange gentleman,' replied Finn, lying with a facility that surprised him. 'Honest, mister.'

'Well,' said Dando, believing him, 'I will not slit your gullet. Nor spread your tripes in a steaming heap upon this highway.' He retrieved his mount and climbed up stiffly, cursing the raw-boned nag for having a head like a lantern and a mouth of iron. 'I am off to Condent Castle, just a social call; I will be staying at the Condent Arms. In consideration for my sparing your life you must report to me the instant you see any strange gentleman. Do you promise?'

Finn nodded.

'Break your word and I break your body. If you are true I will shower thee with ducats, buckets of ducats. Here – ' he tossed the shilling to Finn who caught it neatly, 'that is on account.'

He touched his hat and leered at Cissie who had reappeared around the hedge. A savage wrench of his steed's head, and he was gone.

'A man like that don't have friends,' observed Cissie. 'I wonder what his game is. What's ducats, Finn?'

'Fancy talk,' said Finn, looking at the coin in his hand; not thinking it.

'When he come out of the ditch I thought it was Old Nick himself,' she admitted. 'That's why I ran away.'

'Old Nick?' He repeated the words.

'Ssh!' she put a finger to his lips. 'Speak of the devil and he'll come and stand behind you.'

'Cissie,' Finn closed his hand over the coin, 'do you remember telling me that the Condents came out of Ireland same as myself?'

'Aye, Grammer says they be upstarts. Not been here over a hundred years. There's been Creech's in these parts since the days of the Bible, Grannie says.'

34

'And there's only Lady Condent left. Her son died young out in Ireland. What was his name again?'

'Allan.'

'Yes,' said Finn, watching the dark figure of Dando disappear, 'that's what I thought. Allan Condent.'

CHAPTER FOUR
Fenians Beware

Fenian was the word in every mouth. Kelly and Deasy were spotted in Nottingham, in Liverpool, and in Glasgow, all on the same day; which was impossible. The Manchester police hauled in all the O'Flynns, O'Hallorans, O'Flahertys, O'This, O'That they could lay their hands on; not to mention the Murphys and the Kellys. An Irish accent was enough to excite suspicion. Biting the hand that fed them. Why weren't the Irish grateful? That the same hand had not lifted a finger as the Irish starved to death two decades before was an irony which did not go, in some quarters, unremarked.

Question was – what would the Fenians do next? Something in the violent gunpowdery line, no doubt. But when? where? All over the country from Carlisle to Cornwall, special constables were sworn in to deal with the menace. Earlier in the year there had been an attempted rising in Ireland, but now the enemy was within. By and large they earned their living with the spade, drank too much, spoke with comical accents and lived off potatoes – it was the failure of the potato crop in the forties which had brought them here. And any one of them could be a sworn Fenian, sworn to explode the British Constitution and murder us all in our beds. You couldn't trust them. This wasn't their country. Didn't ought to be here.

Which is what they were saying in the 'Condent Arms' in Monkton. What was Vellew thinking of, bringing in an Irishman to work the mill? That Dermot Hagan could not be trusted, he was a close one, Dermot was.

'Dang me,' cried a farmer, clapping his mug to the table for emphasis, 'if I won't have my corn ground elsewhere!'

Marcus Everett came in. He waited for his beer to be drawn and then joined the group. A man to treat with caution, Marcus.

36

Behind those sandy eyelashes and lazy manners lay an awkward customer.

He blew his froth thoughtfully. 'That Dermot Hagan,' he said, and the group fell silent. 'I heerd you all talking just now as I come in.' He caught the eye of the farmer and held it for a moment, mocking. 'He is just about the best gaffer I ever had. The sort of gaffer a chap could have a fight for.'

He took a pull at his beer while a look passed around the room. They might all be patriots but they weren't all heroes.

The farmer cleared his throat.

'That parcel of land Vellew was selling t'other day,' he said eventually. 'There was a pretty piece of timber on yon.'

But that night someone daubed FENIANS BEWARE in giant letters on the double doors of Dermot's barn.

Dermot chuckled as he examined it next morning.

'Night work.' He went to the outhouse where he kept his whitewash. 'It's the drink makes 'em brave. They haven't the belly to be properly cruel. They could have fired the thatch and cooked us all in our beds if they really meant it.'

Finn stared at the jagged writing which had dripped all down the doors.

'You aren't afraid?' asked Dermot.

''Course I am not.' He was, and the worst of it was that Dermot could tell.

'No need to be afraid,' said Dermot, slapping on the whitewash with a careless hand. 'They are a mild people hereabouts.'

A low mist filled the valley. It was a milky morning; clumps of trees like islands in a stream. The mill and all its buildings looked like ghosts of themselves. A ghostly day; also the first day of school. Mr Tipson had wasted no time.

'He was there in Manchester, wasn't he?' asked Finn. 'Allan Condent?'

Dermot looked up at him from beneath shaggy brows.

'If you mean our visitor of the other night, the gentleman was not free with his name,' he pointed the brush at Finn, it dripped spots of white on the ground. 'Manchester is a great city. Many people come and go and no one thinks anything of it. So don't you think of it. Much less speak of it.'

Finn let the subject rest. 'Look at the mist. It makes everything unreal.'

Dermot grunted and continued his work, a great white blotch against the withered doors of the barn. 'Fenians,' he said with contempt. 'As if the poor yokel who wrote those words had any idea what it meant.'

'No more have I,' said Finn.

Dermot glanced at the kitchen door. 'I promised never to speak of such things to you. Your mother says it is the cause of half our trouble. Yet the word is on everyone's lips – '

He squatted back on his heels, wiping away the paint that had worked down the handle from his fingers.

'Long ago,' he said slowly, 'long ago in the proud days, the far off days, there were men who fought to keep Ireland free. They were called the Fianna. The Fenians named themselves after them. The leader of this band of warriors was Finn Mac Cool.'

Finn's hand strayed to his hair, as it had the night Allan Condent had spoken to him.

'Yes, you have his name.'

'Allan . . . the gentleman told me about him. How he could down a deer on his own bare feet.'

Dermot shifted his view so that he too looked out over the valley. It seemed to Finn that they had never spoken together quite in this way.

'It is my thinking, Finn, that these stories do not always help us Irish.' He laid his brush carefully over the bucket that held the whitewash. 'Look at the mist . . . soon it will fill all the valley and then we will see shapes, such shapes as do not belong in this world. Trees will become giants; strange beasts will crouch in the bracken. It is, as you were saying, unreal. Some Irishmen, when they look back over their history see shapes and figures, giants and beasts, fantastical creatures who take their forms from dim memories. So men with guns name themselves after the Fianna and glory in the bloody business of killing. Those dreams will be the death of many a poor soul – Irish and English alike. Your mother's thinking is the right way.'

'You are not a Fenian then?'

38

Dermot picked up the brush once more. 'I am not,' he said. 'Though I am as big a fool as the next man.'

'But he is – Allan Condent is,' Finn felt he could not get his breath. 'You love him.'

'Well now,' replied Dermot placidly, 'if you are so smart as to know a thing like that – and God knows you have the truth of it – you are smart enough to keep your mouth shut.'

'I did. There was a man asking questions – George Dando was his name – he said he was a friend of his though he lied. He asked me if I had seen him but I told him nothing.'

'A dangerous man. A man who earns his money by selling other people's secrets,' said Dermot. 'But he is gone now. They say that when he was drunk he would speak Shakespeare for an hour together – better than a play he was, they said. He has gone now. We are safe. But now you must be going to school.'

Finn looked back at Dermot kneeling by the barn door; like a warrior himself, great strong forearms, thick fair hair and a beard. 'I won't tell anyone.'

He didn't see Cissie along the way to school, though the ways were thronged with twos and threes of children making their unaccustomed journey; some came because they had been sent, others out of curiosity, others still from a love of learning. For all of them the topic of conversation was the new master and his walking sticks.

Finn's thoughts were still with the Fenian, Allan Condent. His mother said he was in France, but he still wondered if they would meet again. He had been so anxious that Finn would make a good impression with Lady Condent; Finn could understand neither this, nor why his own parents had been in league with him over it. There was another reason, harder to express. It seemed to the boy that he had known Allan Condent somewhere before. But this was ridiculous; he had no memory of either the name or the face.

Around the school gates lounged a knot of boys; chief among them Barty Purvis. Barty was a leader and something of a bully, though so far he had not bothered with Finn.

'Hey, Finnie!' His hair was the colour of stubble and sprang out from his head as if it had been mown. His blue eyes were round and full of a perpetual surprise. 'Have 'ee seen thik new master?'

He ambled into the schoolyard, his limbs bent and shaking in a cruel parody of Tipson. His followers capered in his wake, roaring their approval.

'Screwmaticks,' explained Barty, putting a hand to the small of his back. 'Legs as bent as a knackered old hoss.'

'I think he could be watching you,' replied Finn shortly. A figure moved away from the schoolroom window.

Barty sprang upright. 'It don't matter,' he said, when he was satisfied that no retribution was to fall. 'We aim to make a game of this master same as we did the last.'

'I should watch yourself, Barty.'

'No one lays a finger on Barty Purvis. If he do Father will hear of it.' Barty's father was Monkton's bad lot; he had been to jail more than once. 'No one hits me. 'Cept father, of course,' added Barty. 'He's allus hitting me. Hey, Finnie!'

Finn was taking his place in the line. 'What's your father a going to blow up next? He's one of they Irish Fenians an't he?'

The school bell began to ring, signalling the start of Mr Tipson's reign as village schoolmaster.

'He could always do here,' said Barty hopefully.

CHAPTER FIVE
Mr Tipson

As they filed in, all the children's attention was for the new master. He was seated at his desk beneath the arch of the window. When they came in he lifted his head and they dropped their eyes to the walking stick which lay across the desk before him.

Boys to the left, girls to the right. Finn found himself near the bottom of the class with Cissie opposite. Barty and his cronies were behind him along the back row.

Mr Tipson rose after the roll had been called. The children stared at him with the honest curiosity of rustics. He allowed them a long moment before he spoke, letting his eyes range the rows of faces before him.

That his body was crooked, one shoulder noticeably higher than the other, was undeniable. But his face compelled them; his features were strong, nose rather hooked, a shock of steely grey hair which did not lie flat but ruffled as he moved his head. Like a wild bird, Finn decided; an impression reinforced by the clearness of his eye.

Tipson leant on his stick and calmly scrutinised every face before him. The boy who had so entertained his friends with impressions of himself was in the back row; his hair on end like bleached straw. He was staring at Tipson with eyes that were round and blue. The other boy, also fair haired but possessed of much finer features, sat in the row in front; his cheeks faintly touched with colour as if aware of the teacher's scrutiny; a sensitive young soul. The girls wore drab dresses, dark stockings and black boots; the dullness of it all being relieved by their print pinafores.

Tipson cleared his throat, 'I was going to say something about this being a new dawn. I had a stirring speech prepared along the lines of Shakespeare's *Henry V* but – ' here he paused, and Finn thought he observed a twitch about his mouth, 'I forget it. Suffice it to say that the room has been whitewashed, we have been given a new picture by Mr Pinecoffin depicting Moses in the land of Midian – that is Moses in the yellow robe – and we have, thanks to Lady Condent, a new globe. And *new* benches. I understand the old ones met with an accident. My name, if you do not already know it, is Mr Tipson. There – ' again the twitch about the lips – 'that is the business of introductions done with. Now, bow your heads and ask God, who hears our prayers, to bless our work.'

Then he set them to it; without fuss or undue haste. Barty was given no opportunity for mischief, being kept too busy ciphering. The only break in the morning came with the arrival of Lady Condent and her attendant, Mr Pinecoffin. Lady Condent came to exhort them to their best efforts. Mr Pinecoffin reminded them that God was after them. He was in this very room listening to the very words he spoke, looking over their shoulders when they wrote anything. He always knew and took note if they got up to anything; so they had better Watch Out.

He was received in fearful silence. Lady Condent's chaplain was lately come from London and still a novelty. Though he was beautifully dressed his accents were somewhat common, though only Tipson might note this. When his homily was over he clapped Tipson upon his crooked back and enquired heartily if he had enough coals and newspapers. After a few words they came to an agreement on the subject of newspapers and the visitors withdrew.

'Mister,' Barty's dirty paw waved over the hubbub of tousled heads as the dinner break clattered to an end. 'Me and my mates been thinking.'

Barty was making up for lost time; no opportunity for devilment had come his way that morning and he had even been required to do some work. It wasn't good enough. 'We been thinking about God,' he simpered blandly.

Finn exchanged glances with Cissie; Barty and his chums had spent their break in a corner of the yard plotting. They hadn't even bothered to push anyone over in the mud, or to make the younger ones cry by taking their caps away.

'God. Lord God Almighty,' Barty said piously, raising his eyes to the ceiling while someone sniggered audibly. 'Mr Pinecoffin said He was everywhere this morning.'

'Indeed,' Tipson replied carefully. He was aware of a stillness in the room yet sat sedately at his desk looking at the wide-eyed Barty gently. 'He did say that.'

'Everywhere,' repeated Barty earnestly, with the air of one who wanted to know. 'Everywhere? You mean here in this room? In the air? In the desks? Even in the inkwells?'

'Hardly,' said Tipson. 'Though – '

His qualification was cut short by Barty clapping his hand over the inkwell. 'I've catched God!' he cried and burst into a great horse laugh. He stood up and brandished it aloft. 'Mr Pinecoffin said it! I've catched Good God Almighty – '

There was a concerted gasp at this effrontery, mingled with a sense of awe. Surely Barty Purvis would be struck down dead for this sacrilege. One of the girls, Betty Swallow, told him so. Nothing happened.

'Do you want a look?' enquired the incorrigible Barty. 'Penny a go.'

The gauntlet had been fairly flung down. Every head turned to see what the new master would do now. All except one. Finn was burning with anger; Barty was spoiling everything. He wanted to bring the school back to what it had been before the Inspectors closed it.

'Oh do sit down, Barty,' he cried abruptly, and turned and shoved Barty backwards. The inkpot flew into the air flicking a string of blots along the newly whitened walls. Barty was over-turned but scrambled to his feet at once, his lips fixed into a snarl. Normally he had nothing against Finn but he must be taught a lesson. He had no business shoving his nose where he wasn't wanted. This was between him and Tipson. He got as far as making a fist before finding himself fixed to the wall by Tipson's stick.

Boots clumped noisily on to the wooden forms as the bolder children scrambled excitedly on top of the desks to see what was happening. The teacher had moved with surprising speed down the aisle and now pinned Barty with the point of his stick.

'Thi's hurting my chest,' said Barty weakly.

Tipson leant forward. His face was implacable; his face was so close Barty could see a yellowish rim about the pupils of his eyes. Barty attempted to meet his gaze but failed miserably.

'Thi's hurting.'

Slowly the stick was lowered. Tipson leant on it and regarded Barty.

'Stand up.'

Barty straightened warily; his expression was of utmost surprise. Tipson signed for the children on their desks to sit down. They obeyed at once.

'You have spoiled the wall,' said Tipson.

Barty was dumb; his eyes wide and staring.

'You have made a mock of things which should be treated with utmost respect.'

He moved towards Barty who cowered back warily, arms raised to ward off further blows. 'You are altogether a most promising young villain, destined to end your days dancing at a rope's end – and that in the not too distant future. You are not even original. Well, we will have to take you in hand – '

He turned on Finn, 'Another time you would do well to remember that I am master in this room.' Finn flushed; stung by the rebuke.

With a gesture of contempt Tipson stumped back to his place, leaving Barty half-crouching by the wall. 'The wall must be made good,' he said, turning round. 'Where are you going? Go back to your place.'

'Not I.' Barty had made for the door. 'I'll no more of this school. Father shall hear of this I promise 'ee, Mr Tipson – '

'Lord,' cried Betty Swallow, as the door closed on Barty. 'I hope old Purvis be dead drunk and can't be raised, I do. He is worse nor an animal, drunk or sober.'

'Do I have any more humourists in front of me?' enquired Tipson. There was an uneasy shuffling of feet along the back row where a rough jeering had been the first thing to greet Barty's announcement. Not one head was lifted to meet Tipson's eye.

'Then may I presume,' said that gentleman, 'that the rest of the afternoon may pass in peace?'

He almost had his wish. For the rest of the time the children bent their heads to their work, scarcely venturing a glance at one another. Tipson slowly unbent; towards the end of the afternoon when the monitors had gathered in all the books and they sat with their hands on the desks so he could see them, he began to read to them.

'"Whether I shall turn out to be the hero of my own life, or whether that station will be held by anyone else, these pages must show ..."'

Half-way down the first page any lingering memory they might have had of Barty Purvis was obliterated. The way he read *David Copperfield* was better than a play. They were transported one and all to the Rookery, Blunderstone, Suffolk, on the night of David's birth. Awaiting this event with them was David's aunt, Betsy Trotwood, fully expecting the baby to be a girl; Mr Tipson read her part in a gruff, pugnacious voice which started ripples of laughter. When she took her bonnet and beat the doctor over the head with it, the ripples gathered into a generous wave.

''T'idn't fair,' said Betty to Cissie, in a loud aside. 'The pore doctor couldn't help what the mother threw out – boy or girl. If th'old baggage wanted a girl that bad she should have had one herself when she had the chance.' She folded her arms and sniffed.

Tipson looked up and put a finger to his lips.

Just then the schoolroom door was thrust open.

'I'll knock his face off,' cried a loud, threatening voice. 'I will. Where is he? Show me him – '

Into the room came the sire of Barty Purvis. It was Barty thirty years on; the straw coloured hair greasy and unkempt, the blue eyes cloudy and bloodshot. A dirty, foul-smelling, mean-faced, foul-mouthed individual. Behind father came Barty himself, none too sure whether to smirk in triumph or to flee the scene. He compromised by coming half into the room and leering at his mates.

'Where is he?' demanded the thick-tongued Purvis senior

45

again; though the question was purely rhetorical as he had come up with a bump against Tipson's desk. 'Show me the man.'

'It is not usual to walk in without knocking,' said Tipson, looking at him for the first time. 'But as you are here, sit down and let me finish.'

'You ... you schoolteacher,' Purvis made a wild unsteady motion with his hand in the air. 'You ... you crab!'

He put as much venom as he could muster into the insult and appeared infuriated when Tipson looked merely puzzled.

'Hitting with sticks,' said Purvis darkly. 'Hitting my boy with sticks.'

'He should have been dealt with a good deal more firmly when he was younger, in my opinion.'

'In your opinion,' sneered Purvis. 'Who cares a tinker's damn for your opinion? I don't give *that* for your opinion – ' He attempted, unsuccessfully, to snap his fingers in the teacher's face, tried once again, then gave it up in disgust. 'I've come here to teach you a lesson schoolteacher – I've come to pay you back.'

Barty inched into the room and sneered around at everyone. Hitting with sticks indeed. Now they would see something.

Tipson got to his feet with a sigh and limped around the table to face Purvis.

'I'll give you a thrashing schoolmaster.'

'I think not.'

'You hit my boy, my Barty. I am here to repay that blow!'

One or two of the infants began to whimper.

'Well now,' Tipson thrust his face foward. 'Take your blow. Hit me.'

Purvis senior appeared visibly disconcerted by this novel approach.

'I know your game,' he growled, glancing nervously at Tipson's stick. 'Get me off balance then hit me with *that*. You don't fight fair. I'm up to all your tricks.'

'There's no trick,' Tipson replied calmly.

'Don't think I'm afraid to,' Purvis bellowed, raising his fist.

'I am certain you are not. Go on.'

Purvis looked wildly about at the watching children; every eye was on him and their stare was hostile. It wasn't meant to go this way at all. He became uncomfortably aware of what a poor figure he cut.

'I'm telling you, I will!'

'Very well. Do it.'

Purvis ground his teeth in frustration. 'You don't fight fair!'

'I don't fight at all.'

Purvis shook himself like a goaded animal. Tipson chuckled in a dry, rasping way. Purvis opened his hand and slapped him across the face. An angry blotch leapt in the schoolmaster's cheek and a concerted gasp escaped the children.

Tipson did not even put his hand to the spot.

'You didn't ought to have laughed,' mumbled Purvis.

'I apologise. I was thinking how absurd this was.' Tipson limped with the unresisting Purvis to the door.

'You didn't ought to have laughed,' repeated Purvis senior, abjectly. He stopped before the door. 'Bill Purvis is the name. I am generally to be found about the Condent Arms should you wish to summons me.'

'There will be no summons. Though you would do better to stay away from the Condent Arms and take that son of yours in hand.'

'Where is he?' demanded Purvis with a return of irascibility. He glared at Barty who wore an expression of even greater astonishment than usual. 'You great staring calf, this is all your fault. We have been dragged down lower than ever – look what you made me do! You have made a fool of me.'

He aimed a kick at the nimble Barty who eluded him and the two of them made off with the fond parent in pursuit.

'Well,' said Tipson as he closed the door behind them, 'An eventful day.'

'Why didn't he hit him with his stick?' asked Finn of Cissie on the way home.

'He didn't have to,' replied Cissie wisely.

'I don't see that. He wasn't afraid of him – why didn't he fight him?'

'Men,' said Cissie, from the depths of her twelve year old

experience. 'Always wanting to fight. As if fighting was ever any good for anything.'

'But he insulted him,' said Finn. '*And* struck him. Why didn't he strike back?'

But Cissie laughed at him and would say no more.

CHAPTER SIX
A Fight

Dermot Hagan did not expect much from Monkton's anti-Irish sentiments. A few loads of grain sent to other millers, sheepish attempts to cut him as he made his way along the High Street. But until Vellew came along on his grey cob that was all; that and the great white blot on the barn door.

'They'll tire of it soon enough and come back with their tails between their legs,' grunted Dermot.

Then pale little Vellew came down to the mill and without dismounting told him his rent would be doubled for the coming year.

'God Damn,' Dermot replied. 'I'll see you in the river first my fine man.'

As ill luck would have it there were two witnesses to the scene, wheelwrights fixing the big wagon. They laid their tools aside and listened quietly until Marcus came along and prodded them back to work.

'It was an ugly thing,' Finn's mother told him. 'Two who should be friends. Ice in their eyes and hard mouths.'

She was plunging the heads of cut roses into a basin of cold water then arranging them into a jug. All her movements were dreamy and placid now, her child was big in her. 'It will be Michaelmas soon. Michaelmas is rent day.'

Finn watched a droplet fall from the petal to the leaf and run down the jug like a tear; all the light in the world seemed to be in the drop.

His mother had been blackberrying that morning. The pie was ready for the oven. She picked it up with a cloth and walked over to the black kitchen range.

'Cissie says you mustn't eat blackberries after Michaelmas. The devil has touched them.'

49

'Cissie's head is stuffed with goblins and devils – she could be Irish with all the nonsense that is in her. When she is older she will learn we have enough to worry about without carrying a headful of stories.'

'I thought Vellew was our friend. Why does he want us out?'

'I do not believe he does. The poor man was sore ashamed and did not once look me in the eye. He said twice he was only the agent.'

'For Lady Condent. She has taken against me.'

'I suppose so.' She clanged shut the door of the oven and straightened with a sigh.

'Ma, why did I go to tea with Lady Condent?'

'He – We, wanted you to meet her.'

'Why, Ma?'

She came back to the table humming softly to herself. She moved the roses an inch to one side and stood contemplating them.

'Why, Ma?'

She brushed the fair hair from his eyes. 'See how big you are grown,' she said. 'As tall as your mother already.' She stroked his hair, marvelling how the light touched it so richly. 'How I loved you when you were a baby. I was as proud as a queen when I held you.' Finn blushed and grimaced but stayed where he was. 'But now it is coming to an end,' she added sadly.

'What is coming to an end?'

'Ask no questions, Finn. Hard though it may be for you – you will be told everything soon. We were only doing what someone else wanted us to do.'

'Allan Condent?'

'Dermot told me you guessed.' She picked up her jug of flowers. 'I will tell you this and I will tell you no more.' She moved away to go upstairs. 'We came here to Monkton because he wanted it. You met Lady Condent because it was his wish.'

Finn left the house not knowing where he was going. He would call for Cissie, or perhaps he wanted to be alone; he didn't know.

At the head of the track, looking back along the valley, he could see the waters of the Bristol Channel and the sky mist greyly together. In the heart of this mass lay a speck which moved towards him. He waited while it drew closer and steadily took shape; a grey bird from the grey distance, flying an unwavering line towards him. Now he could hear the powerful wing beats, like rowers, striking a rhythm through the air. He lifted his face and at the same moment the heron uttered a harsh, metallic cry as it flew overhead. Allan Condent, he thought with a thrill, Allan Condent come for me, his shadow passing over me.

There was a wall close at hand which sheltered a well that provided a ready source of fresh water for the cottagers hereabouts. Here were some boys with buckets throwing stones at one another. They broke off at his approach.

'What is it you want, Barty?'

Barty had planted himself in Finn's path, a lieutenant at each shoulder. 'Well now,' he said, licking his lips. 'We have a score to settle. Me and you have to fight.'

Finn looked at each one in turn. 'Let me go by.'

Barty spat at the ground at his feet. 'You shouldn't have pushed me, Finnie. This is a fight for me and you. These two aren't in it.'

Barty's mates cleared themselves and their buckets out of the way to give the contestants room. They were grinning.

'You an't afeard?' enquired Barty seriously, blue eyes wide open. 'You'm Irish. Father says the Irish always want to fight. 'Tis the only straight thing about them.'

'He'd rather be laying under a hedge with Cissie Creech,' suggested someone.

Barty sniggered, 'That's so?'

He stepped back, taking Finn's fist fairly harmlessly on his forehead. With a grunt he aimed a blow in return which Finn, in his turn, narrowly avoided.

'Fight! Fight!' chanted Barty's mates drumming on their buckets for emphasis.

Finn's face was white, his eyes, under the mop of fair hair, like flecks of ice. He held his fists high, the bony knuckles showing white beneath the skin.

Barty blinked stolidly, stepping forward, swinging another blow at Finn's head. Finn twisted away and it missed, glancing his shoulder. Barty's left fist was not so ineffective; he came closer, taking advantage of Finn's loss of balance and jabbed him in the mouth. It sounded like someone smashing an apple. Finn felt only a numbness and the metal taste of his own blood.

There was no pain, only a strange sense of elation. He even felt kindly disposed towards Barty, as if now that the moment for blows had come they could be friends. With a cunning that surprised him he let his fists fall, shaking his head as if to clear it. Barty rushed forward with a growl, arms raised to encircle and grapple Finn, to drag him to the ground. At the last moment Finn swayed aside and brought his fist up into Barty's face.

It was Barty's turn to shake his head, the bright blood appearing at his nose, knees buckling. With a supreme effort he kept his feet and began circling Finn once more. Finn came at him with a straight right and a short left to the body that sent Barty stumbling in amongst the buckets, kicking out and cursing for more room. Finn stayed his ground coolly, fists raised; waiting for Barty to come back to him. The elation was chased quite away by now. He wanted to finish Barty.

Barty was worried; he came back warily, the wide eyes blinking rapidly. Finn went for him with the ferocity of a wild cat, fists flailing from all directions at once. Barty took two more blows to the head, almost tripped once more, then while staggering backwards released a wide clubbing blow with his right hand that dumped Finn on his backside in the dust. Finn's head exploded with light. He scrabbled on all fours, attempting to rise, but his limbs would not obey him. Barty remained where he was, panting and bleeding from more than one place, unable for the moment to do anything to seal his victory.

'Here's Mr Tipson!' cried one of Barty's lieutenants during this lull. 'I'm off!'

The schoolmaster was coming down from the wood, hat to the back of his head, ambling with that lurching gait which had already become familiar about the village. Barty's mates gathered up their buckets and ran off, clanking, to the sanctuary of the cottages. Barty himself took a long look back at Tipson and then at Finn who was sitting up, one eye fast closing.

'Th'art a pretty fighter, Finnie,' he said grudgingly. 'But I

52

reckon I'm paid back for that push you gie me t'other day.' Then he too, though at a more leisurely pace, left the scene.

Finn's head was throbbing. His eye was puffy and he could scarcely see out of it. He stood up sheepishly.

Tipson looked at him with disdain. 'You might well wear that hang-dog look. Was that my friend Barty Purvis?'

Finn could see no advantage in evasion. He nodded.

'And you are Finn Hagan, the Irish boy, the brave lad who fights the schoolmaster's battles for him,' growled Tipson. 'Was this too my quarrel? Or do you fight with Barty Purvis from habit? Or a matter of politics, perhaps?'

Finn flushed; he shrugged in reply, not knowing how to answer this sally.

'And did you resolve the matter?' pursued Tipson angrily, pushing his wild bird's head forward at Finn, all hooked nose and bright eyes. 'Did fighting mend it, you little fool?'

'I think so,' muttered Finn.

'You think so,' Tipson repeated scornfully. 'You think so. Get this into your hot head and keep it there. Fighting never resolves anything except who is the stronger or the luckier. Nothing else. It has nothing to do with who is in the right.'

Finn shrugged once more, his eye was quite closed by now. 'He paid me back.'

'He paid you back – for the push you gave him in school? Well – ' Tipson softened, he lifted Finn's face up and studied the swelling around his eye, 'I should say you have been repaid with interest. Follow me, I will find someone to bathe that eye.'

He stumped away down the path.

'Thank you sir, but I might as well go home.'

'You might as well do as you are told.' Tipson turned and stared coldly at him. 'I was not asking your view of the matter.'

CHAPTER SEVEN
The School House

The school house was at hand. As Tipson led him in through the back way Finn was astonished to see Purvis senior in the yard splitting logs.

'Easy,' said Purvis, with a shamefaced attempt at a sneer. 'I never seed easier logs to split. It's as good as a day off is this.'

'You have done a deal of work,' replied Tipson calmly. 'And I am grateful.'

'Yer,' said Purvis, and he laughed derisively then scowled at Finn. He was embarrassed.

'Came asking to be "took up",' said Tipson, when the door was closed and the woodcutter out of earshot. 'Indignant because I wouldn't summons him. "It'll have to be paid off somehow," he told me – in the end he set to on my logs. I'm truly grateful.'

There was a remarkable untidiness in Tipson's dwelling. The trouble was books; spilling from their few shelves into the chairs, along the floor and into the passage where they made dishevelled piles; on the table, along the top of the piano, leaping on to the mantleshelf where they staggered, exhausted, against one another. Abandoned here and there were items of crockery; an empty teacup on this pile, its companion saucer two yards away, as if Tipson wandered among his mounds of books consulting them while he ate and drank. On the table, its leaves newly cut with a knife which still bore the traces of the morning's toast, was a new volume. Perhaps, thought Finn, gazing at the crumbs around the book, he eats them.

'Mrs Sully should be about somewhere.' Tipson went to the foot of the stairs and called. He listened while the echoes of his cry were ringing around the house. 'Or perhaps,' he said thoughtfully, chewing his lip, 'did she give notice? I seem to remember something.' He opened the door to his sitting room.

54

'It's the books. Show a woman a book and it's odds on she'll want to dust it. I told her to leave them alone but it goes against nature. Fact is, my last quarters were more spacious. I lived in the big house then, lots of bookshelves, never had to think about shelves before. It'll be tolerable when the carpenter has put up the shelves. That's it – ' he held up a finger, 'I remember now, she said if he was coming with his bangings, hammerings and shavings she'd visit her mother in Taunton for a week. Do you know, you're the first visitor I've had?'

An interesting man Mr Tipson. He was the protégé – some said illegitimate son – of the head of a prominent northern family. Despite his disability he had been given a liberal education and the means to travel widely. The summer had been spent among Etruscan tombs. Of late he had been much struck with the ideas of a certain Russian Count with whom he had a lengthy correspondence. Ideas on education and of something else; the non-resistance to evil, pacifism. When Lady Condent had written to his patron and mentioned her need for a teacher, Tipson had begged to be given the opportunity.

The sitting-room smelled brown; a heady whiff of old velvet, tobacco, mouldering bindings; the violin propped in the window seat, dust motes turning over in the afternoon light. Finn sneezed.

Over the fireplace was a picture of several young men in caps holding oars; Tipson was one of them.

'I copied it myself.' The schoolmaster thought Finn was looking at the picture beneath; a naked man with a sling aiming at some birds. 'Etruscan. It was on the wall of a tomb in Italy.'

'I was looking at the photograph, sir. Rowing is it?'

'Yes,' Tipson looked at the photograph and his expression softened. 'I had very strong arms in those days. Water was my element, whether swimming or sculling. It – ' he paused slightly, 'made no difference. Do you admire my views?'

The windows looked into a small orchard and up to the castle on its hill. The turrets showed through the trees, the rooks flew lazily from their perches and back again.

'Lady Condent looks down on me,' Tipson chuckled drily. His ill humour was forgotten now; as was Finn's black eye. He sat down in the window and picked up his fiddle, touching the strings with his bow.

'One of the men in that picture was Irish. There was a song he used to sing which made us cry in our beer. How did it go?' He lifted the bow from the fiddle and hummed to himself. 'What does our Irish miller think of this business in Manchester?' he said.

'Father does not talk of it much,' said Finn cautiously.

'Here,' Tipson put down his violin and began to rummage among a pile of newspapers on the seat beside him. 'Mr Pinecoffin – who has taken me under his patronage – sends me his copy of *The Times* daily. He rarely reads it himself. Here – here is the account I was looking for – "Fenian Outrage in Manchester".'

He thrust the paper at Finn and watched him while he read, touching the strings of the violin, humming to himself, 'Well?'

Finn's feelings were of pride. Pride that ached in his heart. Pride he would do well to hide.

'Did someone walk over your grave? You shudder and have grown quite pale.'

The final part of the account was a description of Allan Condent, "aged 36–40. 5ft 10ins. Hair cropped close. Black whiskers and beard, streaked with grey. Eyes hazel. Stout build. Wearing dark pea jacket, grey trousers, low crowned black hat."

Could he be recognised from that? 'I . . . I wish they had not killed the horse,' he stammered.

'I wish they had not killed the policeman – the one who locked himself in with the prisoners.'

'I have heard it said,' replied Finn carefully, 'that they were only wanting to shoot the lock off.'

'By your father no doubt.'

'Father will not speak of such things.'

'Well, well,' Tipson touched the strings of his fiddle once more, 'does he talk of the years of famine. The Great Hunger? Though it came before you were born so many millions died it must be a topic of conversation in your house.'

'They talk of it but my mother will not allow Father to dwell on it. Black memories breed black hatreds, she says.'

'A remarkable attitude,' said Tipson, and played two or three

56

bars of music. 'I should like to meet your mother. If you want my opinion she is quite correct in her diagnosis – those black memories have bred a generation with murder in its heart. Well, I have remembered the song – it is called Carrickfergus.'

Without another word he began to play. The window was open and the sad sweet music flowed out into the orchard. Slow and sad, the queer crooked figure bent over his fiddle and the melancholy longings of the song escaped out into the evening orchard. Two cottagers on their way home from the wood stopped by the hedge to listen. As Finn listened all the secret pride in his heart turned into a longing whose ache was worse than the first. If only it too, could escape through the open window into the orchard and be carried away by the air.

'There are words too,' said Tipson, as the last notes escaped like a whisper, 'but I forget 'em. My dear boy – ' he laid down his instrument and stared, almost crestfallen, 'bless my soul I had quite forgot – your eye. Forgive me – '

With utmost gentleness he led Finn to the scullery and bathed his eye for him. 'There,' he said. 'And now the both of us have been belted about the chops by Purvis – senior and junior.'

At the front door Finn halted and looked up into Tipson's face. The fierce eyes held no terrors for him now; and there was something which had troubled him.

'You weren't afraid of Purvis that day. Why did you allow him to strike you?'

Tipson returned the gaze of the fair haired Irish boy. 'I want no violence,' he said distinctly. 'If I abhor the fact that Irishmen are killing people on the streets of Manchester, then I must take no part in brawls in my own schoolroom. They are both part of the same thing.'

Finn could make no sense of that. 'I would have hit him.'

'What next?' asked Tipson. 'Would that have put an end to it? What about resentment? Purvis would always hate me – perhaps he would want to fight me again. Don't you see that unless you turn away from such matters they will never end?'

From the back of the house came the stolid sound of wood being chopped. They paused and turned their heads to it.

'Purvis bears me no enmity now – I wish your Irishmen could

say the same. Finn,' he spoke slowly for emphasis, 'listen to your mother.'

Finn shook his head. 'The Fenians are brave men,' he said fiercely. 'I *know* they are.'

'Brave?' He knew as he spoke that the boy would not listen to him. 'There is a higher bravery. "You cannot strike where there is neither fear nor resistance" – Napoleon said those words. They do not have to take to the streets and begin to murder the innocent.'

'They fight for their country,' Finn drew himself up. 'I am wishing I was one of them.'

'No – they fight from hatred, for vengeance.'

Finn walked home, his brows contracted, shaking his head. Tipson was a clever man but odd. There was no sense to what he was saying this time.

Behind he could hear the strains of a violin on the evening air and could imagine the teacher sitting in his seat, thinking his crooked thoughts.

CHAPTER EIGHT
Spunky Night

Dermot was still refusing to pay the extra rent and Vellew was still asserting that they would be put out. He gave them one calendar month after Michaelmas, in consideration of Mary Hagan's condition, to find either the rent or somewhere else to go.

Finn knew his parents had contacted Allan Condent. He had heard them whispering about sending a letter to France. The extra month was almost over, 'Here we are at Hallowe'en,' said Mary, 'and Dermot has not said a word about paying the money.'

'Spunky night,' observed Finn, digging away at a big turnip with his knife.

'More of Cissie's nonsense.' She made the kitchen a sea of misery with her mop. Somehow, Finn thought, it never felt comfortable when Mother washed the floor.

'Yet my head is filled with nonsense of my own.' She rested her back. There was a fluttering in her belly. Like a bird beating its wings. She laughed at herself for thinking like a girl carrying her first. 'I cannot believe Vellew has it in him to put us out.'

'What did he say?' asked Finn.

'That we must pay up or pack up.'

'I did not mean Mr Vellew. I meant Allan Condent.' Finn did not look up.

She sighed. 'No word. We have had no word.'

He continued scooping the woody flesh out of the turnip. He put a piece in his mouth and chewed it thoughtfully. He would give it a great nose and jagged teeth. A face to frighten the dead.

'Spunky night, spunky night,' he intoned gloomily. 'Gie's a candle, gie's a light.'

'Where are you learning such a dreadful way of talking?' she asked, with some exasperation.

'If 'ee don't, 'ee'll have a fright.'

'Are you going with Cissie tonight? I don't want you to be late – it isn't safe.'

He stared at her. 'I thought Cissie's nonsense didn't frighten you.'

'No more it does. It's our neighbours who worry me – threats painted on the barn door – even if all Dermot does is laugh at them.'

It would be after midnight when he got back. Cissie was determined to watch in the churchyard until midnight.

'There's nothing to be afraid of. Half the village will be out.'

'It only wants Purvis with a gallon of cider in him to settle the Fenian problem in Monkton by throwing you in the river – watch that knife!'

'Mother,' he was making the eye holes and narrowly avoided stabbing his hand, 'why did Allan Condent become a Fenian? Was it because his family came out of Ireland?'

She put the mop down and dried her hands on her apron. 'He saw service there in the army,' she replied briefly, 'during the years of the Hunger.'

'Were those really bad times?'

'I myself have seen bodies in the ditch – women and children both – dead of starvation and their mouths green. Yes, green with the grass and weeds they ate to fill their poor bellies. And Allan Condent was a man who came thinking he would help them and found himself evicting the poor creatures from their bit of land. Small wonder he had no stomach for the army. Here – ' her hand was shaking, ' – you will need a bit of a candle to put in that lantern of yours.'

Spunkies are the souls of unbaptized children doomed to wander until Judgement Day. Little Will o' the Wisps that can be seen moving and dancing just above the ground all night. In Monkton Hallowe'en was more commonly known as Spunky Night. It was a night for children, dead and undead; all over the village lights and lanterns danced in the dark while their bearers chanted their rhymes and frightened each other as best they could. It was a night for blackmail:

'My cloe's are very ragged
My shoes are very thin
I've got a little pocket
To put three ha'pence in.

Spunky Night, Spunky Night
Gie's a candle, Gie's a light
If 'ee don't, 'ee'll have a fright.'

Most householders handed over the coppers. If they didn't, well – a lantern left grinning on a gate post was a death threat. No one wanted that, foolish superstition or not.

'But all that is for children.' Finn and Cissie were walking the bare high road, pale under the moon, their lanterns bouncing along like two spunkies come to show them the way to the churchyard. Cissie put her arm through Finn's. The moon grinned down at them from behind a cloud, then went in again. 'There be none of 'em brave enough to come this way.'

Monkton church stood on the high road to everywhere else. There was a handy short cut through the churchyard, much used during daylight. Finn was hoping it wouldn't be too busy tonight. It was surprising how brave he had felt during the day. The church was a massy shadow stacked above the crouching shapes of the yew trees and the roof of the lych-gate.

'In here.' The gate whined piteously. Cissie was most business-like as she led the way in.

'I hope Mother isn't waiting up for me,' Finn whispered, for something to say. The trees chafed and moaned most disagreeably.

Cissie's face loomed up at him, 'You bain't afeard?'

'I am not,' he replied unsteadily. He sighed, 'It's different at night.' In the distance the wind could be heard crashing among the trees on the hill. 'It's so still in here.'

This was all Cissie's doing. Grannie had told her that if you waited by the church gate at midnight on Hallowe'en you could see next year's dead arrive for their funeral. In the daylight even the dreaded Church Yard Walker, whose very breath meant death, was something to laugh at; just one of Cissie's stories.

Now he wasn't laughing. They were here to see if Cissie's grannie came to her own funeral.

As their eyes grew accustomed to their surroundings they could make out humped shapes all around. The tombstones lurched drunkenly, as if all those crammed beneath were grown restless and had begun to toss and turn. He looked uneasily at the face he had carved on the lantern. 'Let's put our lights out,' he whispered.

Once the yellow light was gone they began to feel cold; the night lapped chilly all about them.

'There's sure to be a power of old 'uns come through that gate after midnight,' Cissie's hard little hand crept into his, 'I do hope I don't miss her.'

There was something uncanny about her sure enough. She looked at him and all her dark curls tumbled about her pale face. 'I am grevious sorry, Finn,' she whispered. 'I forgot. I dreamed about you last night. A strange dream.'

He nodded wordlessly and she squirmed nearer, her breath touching his cheek.

'I dreamed I was in a wood sitting on a stump, waiting for someone – I think it was you, Finn. There was a hole in the stump all filled up with black water. I leant over the water and there was your face looking at me. And behind there was a circle, like a crown, in the air.'

'Is that it?' whispered Finn.

'Yes. No. It weren't a frightening dream but saddening. It meant there was a sadness coming to you, it was written on your face. I don't know what the crown meant, though.'

His leg was itching; perhaps there was an ant crawling up it.

'P'raps there might be someone belonging to yourself coming here tonight.'

Finn's reply was cut off by the whirring of mechanism and the rolling iron tones of the clock, rolling across the night like an iron hoop, striking the quarter to midnight.

Cissie stiffened, 'I'm afeard, oh I'm afeard. Will we see the Churchyard Walker? His breath is Death.'

He blew on her neck; she gave a stifled scream and followed it by a sharp kick. It stopped his leg itching. He buried his head in his arms and laughed silently.

They didn't speak much after that. They were side to side, leg to leg, hip and thigh in the dry undergrowth beneath the bush. All down the side of him was warm with Cissie.

'Cissie – '

She turned her face to him, her lips slightly parted. 'Yes, Finn?'

'There an't no one else you like?'

'Only you, dear Finn.' He could see her small teeth gleaming in the dark.

'I – ' The great clock above stirred and whirred and began to clang out the hour of midnight. Cissie pinched his arm so violently he almost cried out.

'Look – !'

Even as the annunciation of the hour rolled through the night a muffled figure was coming through the gate. It stopped next to their bush and groaned.

Cissie buried her head, her fingers tight about Finn's wrist. The figure staggered a few steps, then halted, swaying. 'Oh, Jesus,' it said. 'Oh, Judas.'

Finn gazed, eyes wide with fright, the skin prickling all over his body.

The figure sighed and turned to face the bush where they lay. His face was swathed in scarves almost up to the brim of his hat. 'Judas,' he repeated in a muffled voice and staggered even nearer. 'I am damned.'

Finn could bear it no longer, he sprang up with a noisy crashing of foliage.

'Who's there?' The figure shrank back. 'Have you been following me? Pinecoffin, is that you?'

Finn stepped forward, 'It's myself, Mr Vellew, Finn Hagan.'

To his consternatio.., Mr Vellew, whose voice he had at length recognised, shrank back even further putting his hands up to ward him off.

'Spunky night!' he cried. 'Have you come to haunt me?' Even at this distance Finn could smell the sweet scent of cider on the agent's breath. 'To throw my promises báck in my teeth – to demand justice?'

'It's Finn Hagan, Mr Vellew. I don't understand you.'

'Really you?' Vellew lowered his hands and screwed up his fuddled eyes. 'But I have been tormented in my thinking by you and yourn for so long,' he said pathetically. 'Lend us a grip of your arm.'

Finn did as he was bade. The little agent, gingerly at first, touched it then clasped it ardently with both hands and brought his face richly up to Finn's. 'Real enough,' he sighed. 'Flesh and bone, muscle and sinew, skin and blood. Warm. To think I swore a solemn oath to protect this arm – and the rest of your precious body.'

'I do not understand, Mr Vellew,' said Finn sharply, drawing his head back, much embarrassed by these attentions.

'I promised the young master that I would cherish 'ee. Even though he is no better than a bandit. I swore that I would see you found favour in the eyes of the lady. Oh, Judas – ' He broke off and groaned despairingly. 'I have been false and broke my word. I have been harrying Dermot Hagan so he would take you away.' He drew even closer. 'Forgive me,' he whimpered. ''T'was Pinecoffin put me up to it. I am in his hands – one word from Pinecoffin and I am ruined!'

'I am very sorry for it,' replied Finn, not at all knowing what Vellew was talking about.

'Bless you, my boy,' said Vellew, patting his arm. 'But I don't deserve it. A man who breaks his vow is damned. I know I am drunk but I have not drunk enough to blot out that knowledge. I was thinking of it the very moment I came through that gate, my heart breaking, when you come out on me the good Lord knows from where, at the very moment of my despair.'

He relinquished his hold and straightened, curiously dignified now. He hiccuped. 'Tell Dermot I will see him right in the matter of the rent. I will honour my word to young master Allan though it may be the ruin of me. I shake Pinecoffin off – ' He suited the action to the words and staggered a few paces into the gloom. His sick face, like a Spunky Night turnip, turned to Finn from the shadow. 'This is no place for 'ee, boy. Go home and tell

Dermot what I told you. Myself – ' he made an invisible gesture towards the castle; lights still showed at some of the windows, 'I will not rest until I have spoken to the Lady up yonder. She rises early and I will be waiting for her. Good night, my boy. May God bless you and good fortune follow you.'

The night gulped him whole. He was gone. Finn waited until he heard Cissie move and they both began to hurry along the road to the village, all thought of Grannie forgotten.

'Hurry!' hissed Cissie, 'Can't you be quicker!'

Only when the white walls of the first cottages glimmered at them did she slow her running walk. She gulped for breath, 'I've seen *him*!'

'Vellew?'

She shook her head. 'I saw him. Flitting behind the stones like a big black shadow while you was talking to Vellew.'

Finn turned cold. Someone else?

'The Dark Stranger – The Churchyard Walker! Finn, we have meddled where it an't fitting to meddle. I'm going home to hide beneath the blankets – '

The Creech cottage was at hand. Cissie was gone with a slam of the door and no word further.

The Dark Stranger. The silent street, black with menace, was no place to linger. He began to run. Along the lonely track to the mill he began to feel a shrinking sensation in his back. He whirled around. Nothing. A hedgehog rustled in the verge and he crossed himself, expecting to feel the cold fingers, or icy breath of the Churchyard Walker caress his neck. But there was nothing.

On the gate posts of the mill, winking and grinning wickedly at him, were not one, but two, three turnip lanterns. It took all his courage to knock them off and crush them underfoot.

With one last look over his shoulder he took a deep breath and opened the kitchen door.

Sitting there, feet on the hob, was the Dark Stranger himself. Allan Condent.

CHAPTER NINE
The Mill Wheel

'You are shivering. Are you ill?'

He swung his feet down and faced Finn, spectacles glinting in the firelight.

Finn swallowed, hand still on the latch, 'Was that you in the churchyard when I was talking to Vellew?'

Allan Condent's face was full of shadow. 'Not I,' he said. His hair was grown longer; Finn could see that his beard was dyed darker, the distinctive grey markings were gone. 'I have been waiting for you for the past two hours. Dermot and Mary are in their bed. Come and sit down, your mother left bread and milk for you.'

Finn slid into his seat at table and poured milk into a cup setting the jug down slowly and carefully. Condent watched him, hands thrust up the sleeves of his coat like the first time. It was a different coat, though. He wore a well cut tweed.

'I am a gentleman on a walking tour,' he said, following Finn's eyes. 'I have to look the part.'

'I saw Vellew. He said he would put the business of the rent right. We do not have to move.'

Condent inclined his head, 'Then mine is a wasted visit.'

'I know all about you,' said Finn.

'So Dermot tells me. How did you know?'

Finn shrugged, 'I listen. And I saw the schoolmaster's newspaper. You are Lady Condent's son – the one who led the ambush in Manchester, though the police do not know your name. They are looking for you.'

Allan Condent, still and peaceful, like the dark pools of the river outside, just as dangerous. He smiled and a rare charm transfigured his face.

'Fortunately the police are not as quick as you. When they catch someone it is generally by mistake. They caught Kelly and Deasy

66

because they thought they might be burglars. But what caused Vellew to change heart?'

'He said it was all Pinecoffin. Pinecoffin made him harry Dermot so he would take me away.'

The shadow returned to the face. 'Pinecoffin. The pet chaplain. Well, I will pay Vellew that visit now I am here. I am curious about this man's involvement in our affairs.'

Finn chewed on his crust, washing it down with milk. 'There was a man called Dando. Offered me money for news of you.'

Allan took up the poker, stirring the embers so that the little yellow flames began to dance once more. Someone was shouting in the night outside.

'He is a spy. At this moment he is in Manchester helping the police to arrest all the Fenian sympathisers he can name.'

'He said he was your friend.'

'He has no friends. He is an adventurer of the worst sort, ex-actor, ex-soldier of fortune, spy. We served together during the American War. There were a lot of the Brotherhood in our regiment and Dando attached himself to them and made himself useful to them. He affected to hate the English government. Now he takes its money in return for what he has learned about us. I saved his life once.'

'He was not grateful?'

'He was so grateful he cursed me.' He laid down the poker, put a finger to his lips, and stepped softly to the door, opening it on to a night flecked with stars.

Beneath the poplars on the opposite bank a man punched holes in the empty air and filled them with oaths.

'Purvis,' said Finn at Allan's shoulder. 'He will fight anyone when he has taken a drink. He hit the schoolmaster not so long ago.'

'Poor fellow. Monkton's schoolmasters live dangerously in these days.'

'He was not afraid. He let him. It is what Napoleon would have done . . . at least I think it is what Napoleon would have done.'

In a broken-hearted way Purvis aimed another punch at the empty air and stumbled among the nettles.

'Brimful of anger,' observed Allan softly. 'If this was Ireland I would recruit that one.' They closed the door gently.

67

Back in the kitchen Allan sent Finn on up to bed, 'We will have a talk tomorrow, you and I. I will tell you about myself and we will be friends.'

'Yes,' said Finn. 'Yes. I should like that.'

'My mother's religion was like a coffin.' They were in Finn's room. Allan, after watching Finn take his bowl of porridge, was sitting upon a stool on the bare boards at the foot of Finn's bed.

'Before I go back to France,' he said, 'I want to make your future assured with my mother, Lady Condent. That is why you are here in Monkton. My inheritance is being dissipated between my mother and her odd chaplain. Do you wonder that I should like to help just one person myself? Also – ' he looked at Finn with a gentle light touching his eyes, 'I want you to remember me.'

Finn watched from the bed. Work had begun long ago outside. The rumble of the mill wheel played, unheeded, beneath the steady tone of the Fenian's voice. 'Like a coffin. And an old woman, my nurse – Annie – saved me from suffocation.'

He peered from the window; the river, the fields, the trees, up to where the tower stood plain on its hill. The empty tower that stood on the opposite height. The tower everyone called Condent's Folly.

There flicked into his mind, like an image on a glass lantern slide, a dark bedroom, a sleepy child, an old woman crooning stories in his ear.

'Annie made Monkton Ireland; though it has taken me half a lifetime to see it. This river here was where the great salmon of knowledge swam; the fish that Finn Mac Cool caught and cooked when he was a boy. He burnt his thumb on it when he was cooking it and when he sucked the sore place all the knowledge passed to him instead of to his master who was waiting to eat. Do you know the story? No matter.

'The tower . . . it was there that Finn and his men hung their shields. I have seen them running through those fields in their white war helmets.

'Do you remember I asked you how many poplars stood on yonder bank and you told me seven? They were the seven warriors charmed into the shapes of whispering trees – I used to run down here at night to tell them Finn Mac Cool would soon release them.'

68

He laughed gently, remembering himself, a small boy locked in his own dreams. 'They are waiting still.'

He came and sat against the wall, drawing up his knees and resting his chin on them like a boy.

'. . . So many dreams. I have tried to be rid of them but Annie planted in fertile soil. Can you imagine my feelings when my regiment was posted to Ireland – the Mother Country?'

And he told this boy the story of his life in those days. How beautiful Cork looked when they saw it from the sea. How the people were dying from hunger yet still sending food to England so that the rents could be paid. How his company had to stand guard over a shipment of oats and grain for England in Cork harbour.

And the rest of it: the burnings, the bodies in the fields, destroying houses, the evictions. The last day; when he found a man being eaten by rats.

'There was an old man gathering weeds in a ditch for his family to eat. The look he gave me I have seen only once since – ' Allan Condent shivered, 'it haunts me still. I knew I could wear the Queen's uniform no longer. I was betraying all my dreams – '

Finn laid a hand on his arm, 'It was not your fault. How could you be to blame?' He looked at him and a new understanding filled his heart. 'You have fought ever since. To make up. To make up for all this – ' He waved his hand at the river, the trees, the fields, the tower, 'For all this – '

Below someone burst into the kitchen and ran to the foot of the stairs.

'Finn, come quick. The wheel is snarled.' It was Dermot.

'When things are bad you must fight,' Finn pulled on his shirt and breeches.

'Life is not as simple as one of Annie's stories,' replied Allan. 'But hurry. Do not be keeping Dermot.'

The rains had swollen the river. Upstream the banks had given way and trees sent their branches spinning down with the current to become snagged on outcrops of rock, causing obstructions and further flooding. More than once the mill wheel had stopped, fouled with branches, roots or other rubbish.

'A root, I'm thinking.' Dermot and Marcus were leaning on long poles. 'I saw something dark right beneath the wheel. 'Tis heavy enough. Take a pole now Finn and let's be doing.'

Marcus Everett spat on his hands. 'Now the boy's here we need have no fear.' He shot a sidelong glance at him. 'He been up there writing poems to his lady love.'

Finn blushed, despite himself. 'I wasn't writing poems,' he muttered.

'He be bursting with prowess.' Marcus pronounced the last word slowly and gave a dirty laugh.

'Enough,' grunted Dermot. 'Three together, push!'

The wheel cracked and groaned, but would not move.

'Heave!' The big vein stood out on Dermot's forehead. Marcus' face was expressionless but his eyes glittered with the effort he was making. He winked down at Finn. Finn returned the wink and strained forward with every scrap of his strength. The wheel groaned once more and moved slightly before fouling again.

'Damn it to Hell!' cursed Dermot. 'Just when it begins to move. Go you and take a look, Finn.'

Finn inched forward on his belly among the long grass by the river bank. The water swirled inches from his face, stirring a faint scum beneath the wheel.

'I see it. Something dark right enough – ' he halted abruptly.

Something in his silence warned the men. 'What do you see?' demanded Dermot sharply.

'A boot,' replied Finn, 'I see a boot. It's not moving.' It was a stupid thing to add but the peculiar stillness of the object was terrifying.

The two men exchanged glances and gripped their poles. 'Once more,' muttered Dermot.

Once more and then with an almighty effort once more as the wheel cleared and the current caught in the paddles.

'Christ Jesus,' said Dermot, in awe.

Rising ponderously from the water, one arm hooked through the mill wheel paddle, was all that remained of Mr Vellew, Lady Condent's steward.

CHAPTER TEN
The Verdict

They dragged the body clear. How long he had been in the water wasn't known but the water had washed him fish white. It oozed and drained from him in rivers, making a pool all about his frail twisted form.

'His head,' said Marcus quietly to Dermot.

'Go you in,' Dermot said the Finn. 'Tell your mother what has happened. She will know what to do. Poor Vellew – here,' he took an empty sack and laid it over the upper part of his body, 'we must treat him decent.'

'He was only a little man,' remarked Marcus.

Finn was sent with a message to the castle. Within two hours four uniformed policemen arrived with a van. Marcus, smoking his pipe, watched them take Vellew away.

'Do you remember what you said to him that day when he told you he was putting the rent up?' he said softly in Dermot's ear.

Finn, by the wall, was dropping shreds of fern into the river, listening.

'I wish I had never said it,' replied Dermot. 'For all the man provoked me. Does it look bad for me?'

'As bad as they want it to,' responded Marcus thoughtfully. 'Not a scrap of proof – he must of gone in further up the river but they will not be worried about that.'

Dermot seized Marcus by the shoulder, 'You don't think I was the one – '

'Master, I would not be standing here with you if I thought anything like that,' replied Marcus calmly. 'I expect he fell in. Poor little man.'

'I saw him last night,' said Finn. 'He was drunk.'

'There then,' said Marcus puffing away, 'others must have seen him so.'

71

Next day two of the policemen came back and took Dermot away. For questions.

Finn scrambled up the stairs to where Allan Condent lay, reading a book, gazing up quietly at the tower where Finn Mac Cool had hung his shield.

'There is no evidence to connect Dermot with Vellew's death apart from a few unfortunate words,' he said calmly, after listening to Finn.

'He said he would put him in the river.'

'That is no proof of anything. Besides, I was sitting with Dermot all evening and would swear he never left the house – '

'You!' Finn twisted about in alarm. 'They are waiting to hang you.'

His concern seemed to touch Condent. 'It will not come to that,' he said gently. 'There is no evidence. Poor Vellew fell in the river – you told us how drunk he was.'

Finn felt a small relief easing through him. He too, tried a smile, his first, perhaps, for two days.

'But what about the mark on his head? Father covered him up, but not before I'd seen.'

'It was probably made by a stone or a root after he fell in.'

Below, in the kitchen, Mary Hagan sat by the fire alone with her thoughts. Marcus had followed Dermot to the police station and was waiting outside for news. She had a piece of knitting with her but it was laid by. She was thinking how it was the same as last time. One hand rested on her tight belly, feeling through the thickness of her clothing the quickening of the child within her. She could remember when it was Finn; though then it was a turf fire she had waited by. And even then Dermot and Allan had been with her, and there had been danger too.

'What concerns me now,' went on Allan upstairs, 'is what we are all to do now Vellew is dead. After my mother disowned me he wrote to me secretly saying I could rely on him for any help he could give. He let Dermot have the mill at my request – '

'Why did you do such a thing?' asked Finn quickly.

'So you could be brought to my mother's attention.'

'The tea – '

'Yes, dear Finn. Vellew had been following my interest in this

72

too. Though once more the chaplain, Pinecoffin, stood in our way. The tea, I understand, was not a success.'

'Why me? What am I to you – why have you chosen me to help?'

Condent regarded Finn with affection, choosing his words with care, 'When you were born I was there. You have always had a special place in my regard. It seems hard that I should not be able to help those I choose. Vellew felt he could interest Lady Condent in you with a view – '

'With a view?' repeated Finn coldly.

'To educating you – '

'What is wrong with the education I have?'

'Something more fitting, more gentlemanly – '

'A gentleman? An English gentleman? The very thing you gave up?'

'No.' For an instant the coldness was mirrored in Condent's face. With an effort he mastered it, 'Do not misunderstand me. I wanted to give you something better than the village school, something more permanent than the wandering life you have known so far. But this discussion is wasted. Without Vellew we all waste our time in Monkton – I would never approach my mother, myself. Dermot will wish to be away after the baby is born. You must expect a new baby to take a lot of their attention.'

'Don't I know that,' replied Finn humbly. 'Father is so excited when he talks of it. One would think he never had a child before.'

'I was wondering,' went on Condent, 'whether you would come with me to France. We could accomplish the same object there. You could become a European gentleman – and always an Irishman.'

'France,' Finn repeated the word but no sound came.

'A man may live peacefully there. You could come and see how you like it.'

'Listen,' said Finn, his eyes suddenly dancing with light, 'Father is home.'

Below, in the kitchen, Dermot was wiping away Mary's tears with a horny uncomfortable thumb.

'There,' he said, in a voice that rumbled with tenderness. 'Did you think I would not return?'

She grasped his hand, 'I did not think they would let you go,' she whispered.

Dermot tossed his crumpled cap on to the table and walked to the door that opened on the stairs. 'Bring your friend down a little minute, Finn,' he called. 'The dark is coming on. I will close the shutters.'

'They had Purvis there too,' he said, when they were all gathered. 'Whenever there has been a fight they go to see him. They put us together – there is only the one cell there – we walked part of the way home together.'

'Could he – when he was drunk?' Finn looked at Allan.

'No evidence at all,' said Dermot. 'The schoolteacher rubbed their noses in that one plain enough. He came to our rescue.'

'Mr Tipson,' said Finn proudly.

'Mr Tipson,' agreed Dermot. 'There's a man. 'Tis a pity he's so crooked in the back. Though when he looks at you out of them sharp bird's eyes of his I would not dare feel pity for him. Easy to see why he has tamed the wild men in that school of yours.'

'He rescued you?' said Allan.

'He limped in, leaning on his stick, and enquired how much longer they were going to keep us. He wanted Purvis for a job. If they didn't have any evidence and weren't going to charge us they ought to let us go. *Habeus Corpus*, he said. Sat and waited, cool as you like, humming a tune to himself. So they let us go after asking us the same tom fool questions all over again.' He looked at Mary and then over at Allan. 'No point in staying now, is there?'

Misadventure was the coroner's verdict. Enough people came forward to testify to Vellew's drunkenness. The barman at the Condent Arms had even advised him to take care, being worried about the state of him. He was like a man drinking himself up. 'Drinking himself up?' enquired the coroner over the top of his spectacles, 'What is meant by the phrase?' Couldn't say. 'Getting up his courage, perhaps. To kill himself?' Couldn't say.

Public opinion wanted a more sensational verdict; the more

enlightened, led by Tipson, scoffed at this. Public opinion contented itself by whispering behind its hand. The killer was either Dermot Hagan or Purvis, it said. To a certainty. Possibly both of them. Either way it was best to have nothing to do with them.

Winter came one night and blew the trees naked and shivering. Outside the leaves lay in drifts along the lane. The hills, which had lain like tawny lions in the sun, turned drab and small. The kitchen was full of draughts and the fire smoked.

'So, Allan will take you to France.' The faces loomed above Finn anxiously.

'We are finished here, Finn. We have to move away.' All the pinched anxious faces; winter, sure enough.

Allan Condent buttoned his coat for him as if he were a small boy and they were leaving that instant. 'Think of it as a visit. That's all.'

What about Cissie? Mr Tipson? He frowned; there was no one else to miss. And he would rather be with Allan.

'Can't we all go?' he asked.

'Just the two of us,' said Allan.

Whatever he said was law to his parents. Finn noticed the glance that passed between them.

'Do not fear for him, Mary,' said Allan. 'I will see him safe at the first hint of trouble.'

CHAPTER ELEVEN
The Plot

Allan Condent tossed his newspaper to one side as the train jerked its way out of Taunton.

'They are still talking of Fenians,' observed Finn from the seat opposite.

'And will not be done this year,' replied Allan drily.

'How long will we be in France?'

'George Dando has been busy in my wake, I see.' Allan touched the paper which dealt at length with the trial of some suspected Fenians held in Manchester. 'I have done with it all. My active service is over.'

Finn gazed at him; he was relieved, though a small part of him was disappointed. Allan Condent was a hero in his eyes.

Allan danced his fingers on his knees and looked out of the window at fields, hedges, ditches. Hurrying by, avoiding his gaze.

'In Manchester I shot a horse,' his breath clouded the glass.

'So it was you,' Finn thought of Tipson's room, the picture of the man with the sling, the diamond panes of the window; Tipson touching the strings of his violin while he waited for the boy to finish reading the newspaper, 'I wish you had not shot the horse.'

'If I had not done it the van might have got away; more men would have been killed. What is the death of a horse? It happens every day that some poor brute collapses in harness and a crowd gathers to watch its last agony. Yet . . . do you remember the old man who danced a jig while my soldiers marched into his village?'

'The look he gave you you have only seen once since.' Finn forgot nothing Allan told him.

'As the horse lay dying the driver of the van gave me the same look. I was both feared and despised. I was on the other side yet the fear I engendered was the same. Do you see what I mean?'

Finn shook his head slowly.

'It is all the same,' said Allan. 'Killing is killing whoever commits it. All soldiers are guilty men. I have no faith in killing any more.' Allan's eyes had in them a far away look as if he could not see what passed before them; trees, hedges, ditches. 'Bite your thumb, Finn. Finn Mac Cool bit his thumb when he wished to know the future. Tell me what you see.'

'I cannot see the future.'

'Well, one more small thing in London and then my association with the Fenian brotherhood will be at an end.'

Finn felt happy. Even though he had left Monkton and home behind him.

'We'll have a fine time, I think.'

'Call me Allan.'

'We'll have a fine time of it, Allan.' He swallowed at the pride of it.

The station was lost in gloom when they arrived. Night had seeped beneath its cavernous roof leaving only small pools of light where the gas lamps burned. They descended warily, like voyagers newly come to the other world. Their ears were filled with the sounds of fire and steam; even the cries of the porters sounded as if they were lost and couldn't ever get out.

'Are we safe?'

Allan knew what he meant. 'No one will suspect a man and a boy. Besides they think they have caught everyone involved at Manchester.'

Finn clutched at his arm. Though it was dark there were throngs of people.

'There is some small business to settle. I was to meet them beneath the station clock. It should not take too long. Take this – ' he handed Finn a purse. 'You may watch from here. Should something go wrong – not that it will – you must go to the ticket office and buy a ticket to take you home. Do you understand?'

Finn did not release his arm. 'You said . . . you said you were finished with them. You are meeting them now – here?'

'Do not take on so,' said Allan gently. 'One more small thing, that is all. I swear I will not be gone more than a few minutes. Wait here by this pillar. I do not expect the porter will object if

77

you sit on his trolley for five minutes. There is my clock.' He pointed to where the white face of the clock, like the man in the moon, peered down over the concourse. People passed beneath or stood idly together in knots. 'Trust me.'

Finn watched his upright back as he disappeared into the crowd. He sat on the trolley and huddled into his coat. He felt cold; more than cold, sick and uneasy.

An arm slipped through his; 'Ill met by gaslight,' said a voice in his ear. 'Never forget a face. Last time I saw you, you was engaged in a bout of fisticuffs. In Monkton. Now you are hobnobbing with a gentleman who looks uncommonly like Allan Condent, the notorious revolutionary and fugitive. Rum do. Let's talk – not here neither. Come along.'

Dando tugged gently at him. 'I mean you no harm, coz,' he murmured. 'But I have a persuader in my pocket, should you prove stubborn. Remember how I once promised to spill your tripes on the road? Promise holds good. Besides, I'll let you go back to him once we've talked.'

He gave Finn the benefit of his yellow tooth and propelled him out of a side entrance, grinning down at him like his uncle met him off the train.

'Followed 'em to the station tonight,' he muttered. 'I know where they're holed up. I smell something big coming up – they won't catch me like they did with the Manchester job. I'm in on it this time. Who are they waiting for – Captain Condent, that's who. Where is he taking you?'

'France.' Finn found his voice, they were in the wide street, standing in the light shed by the doors and windows of an imposing hotel. 'He's taking me to France.'

'That horse won't run,' Dando chewed one end of his moustache. 'Won't do at all. The something I can smell is happening here. Try again.'

'It's the truth, Mr Dando. He's finished with them.'

'Tell you that did he? That's why three known Fenians come to meet him?'

Finn looked about wildly for aid. It came from a most unexpected quarter – 'Mr Pinecoffin!' Finn called as down the steps of the hotel came that very person, 'Mr Pinecoffin, sir!'

Pinecoffin, or his double to the life, looked at them and looked away again, signing for a cab. But there could be no mistake, surely.

'To the life,' murmured Dando. 'Am I going mad? Has half Monkton moved up to town? But of course, he is the gent who runs the home for Lady Condent. Begging your pardon,' he said as the servant retraced his steps to the hotel, 'we thought – my young friend and I – that we knew the gentleman who just walked by with you. Was not that Septimus Pinecoffin, in the Bible bashing way of business, runs a home for waifs and strays in Wapping, or somewhere?'

'Bless you, no, sir,' replied the servant affably. 'That 'ere party is too much of a sport to take his religion serious, he is. Not that he ain't grand in his own way, neither. Spends money like nobody's business. Why, his bill for cigars would pay your wages for half a year. Mine too. Stays with us regular, he does.'

'I beg your pardon once again. His name?'

'Can't be any harm in telling you. Not that I can see – Mr Samuel Wentworth, of Somersetshire, I believe.'

'Gratified,' murmured Dando. He brought Finn to an alley by the side of the hotel and they rested in the shadows. 'Small world. And rum. But to return to the business in hand, would you believe me if I promised – '

'No,' said Finn. 'When can I return to the station? He will be missing me.'

'Told you then,' said Dando. 'Told you that I would always keep Condent from arrest – as much as it lies in my power. I am paid for information. The bigger the tip off, the bigger the pay off, if you follow me. But I owe Condent something – the trifling matter of my life – and would not willingly give him up to his death. Tell me where you are going.'

'Why do you spy on him then, if you owe him your life?' said Finn scornfully.

'It's a living. Besides, the game he plays is bigger than himself. He is embroiled with a gang of mad, dangerous Irishmen – '

There was a rustling behind them. 'A rat, a cat,' said Dando, observing the boy's eyes widen. 'Tell me where you are going – '

'Behind you – ' gasped Finn, involuntarily.

But it was too late. A thud and Dando fell forward on to Finn, all his weight gone to slack and heavy like a bag of mill flour. He grunted as he fell on to his face in the alley.

'The captain will be wanting you,' said a small, hard Irish voice.

Finn gazed with horror at his feet where Dando lay crumpled.

'He is killed!' he whispered.

'Very like. And a good thing too.' The Irishman wiped the butt of his revolver on the inside of his coat before hiding it away. He was not an impressive man in regard of height and size; which made him seem, oddly, the more murderous. 'A bullet is too good for the likes of him.'

In the street light his clothes could be seen to be seedy and shabby; his red hair jagged and unkempt.

'Why, you are trembling,' he said, laying a hand on Finn's arm.

Finn drew himself away as if the hand were red hot.

The Irishman laughed, without humour, full of bravado. 'You will come hardened to such sights, bye and bye,' he said. 'There was a time when I would run away from a fight myself. But a gun's a great thing, indeed it is.'

He meant that a little man with a gun was the equal of any man. Finn knew what he meant and knew instinctively that he was keeping company with that most dangerous of creatures, a coward with a gun. He thought of Dando in the alley.

'He was not going to hurt me,' he said, with outrage.

'Bad cess to all informers and spies,' was the answer. 'A clean death does him too much honour. Let him be found among the trash, 'tis only where he belongs.'

Such was Dando's epitaph. Allan, white faced with anxiety, was waiting with two other men. There was a cab standing by. 'You are unhurt?'

'Yes.'

'Thank God for that. Come along.'

They travelled alone through the dark London streets, the others coming on behind.

'That was Desmond. Here – you are cold.' He wrapped his own coat about the boy, kept his arm around him too. 'I thought you were gone. This is a bad beginning,' he said.

80

'Why are we going with these men, where are we going?' asked Finn.

'It is better I do not tell you the name of the place. The less you know, the better for you.'

'That man Desmond. I hate him.'

Allan sighed. Together they watched the street lamps, the dark hurrying figures, so many in this great city, all the multitudes of lights reflected in the water that lay in the streets. They crossed the river and for an interval there was a sensation of space, of air, of sluggish water making its way to the open sea. Then they were plunged into more streets, closer and more narrow.

'They are not all like Desmond,' said Allan, at length.

'Do we travel to France tomorrow?'

Again the sigh. The grip tightened around Finn's shoulders.

'Something has come up.'

After a long time the cab drew up in a street. It was a street in which one house looked much like another; they were boxes rather than houses, rabbit hutches for working men.

An interval away the other cab drew up and the three Fenians descended. Condent led Finn to a door, knocked three times, paused, knocked twice more. It opened on the second knock. 'The others are coming,' he said.

The doorman nodded his head, 'It's yourself, Captain.' His head kept nodding. 'And the fine boy too, a broth of a boy.' His head kept up its rhythmic movement, Finn noticed his hands shook continually too, the lamp was not at all steady.

'Come in, come in,' he sang the snatch of a song under his breath while their shadows jigged along the wall. 'Come in out of the cold, children.'

'They will want to talk straight away,' said Allan quietly. 'You should not be there.'

'Take her away down the quay,' sang the doorman in an undertone. 'I won't marry her at all today. Aha, here come the other brave lads. Come in, boys.' His whole body kept up its continuous rhythm, his hairless head keeping time to the song he sang.

'What is the matter with him?' whispered Finn.

81

'The war,' replied Allan, and in a louder tone, 'Patrick, would you take Finn upstairs. Show him where he can sleep.'

'I will indeed. Toot de sweet,' said Patrick. 'The tooter the sweeter,' and sang, 'She's too tall and I'm too small, I won't marry her at all at all.'

Finn followed behind. Allan watched him up the stairs, the others pushing by without a word, 'Try to rest, Finn.'

Patrick with the nodding head and shaking hands waited by an open door, 'Take her away down the quay,' and as Finn came up, 'That'll be two shilling for the night,' and held out a trembling hand.

Finn was startled. 'I only have a sixpence.'

'Done.' Patrick took it and stowed it in his shirt. 'Have you such a thing as a plug of tobacco for me pipe?'

Finn demurred. Patrick, deciding nothing more was to be gained, showed him the room. A bed, a washstand and a quantity of dust. Finn sneezed.

'The master bedroom,' said Patrick grandly. 'Three of 'em slept here last night, two majors and a captain, give me their boots to clean too, just like a regular army. Economical room. I won't leave a light on account of the street light being conveniently situated outside the window.'

'What war were you in?' asked Finn.

'America,' said Patrick. 'Some terrible bangs in America. In here too,' he indicated his head. 'They've got in here and won't go away. Sing to keep them quiet. Night is the worst.' He shook more quickly.

Somewhat nervously Finn asked how many he might expect to share the bed with.

'They'll talk all night. War council.'

After remarking that the stove pipe in the corner came from downstairs and warmed the room he said good-night.

'I hear guns in my head. Bang. Bang.' His head shook and he laughed, 'But we'll all be hearing 'em soon enough.'

He went off, his shadow jigging alongside him wilder than ever. 'She's too tall and I'm too small, I won't marry her at all at all.'

Beneath him, Finn could already hear the rumble of men's

voices. The thin walls of the cheap house could not disguise the voices though the words were indistinct. He recognised Desmond. Somehow he had thought of the Fenians as handsome and noble like Allan Condent. That they had room for the cowardly and mean was a novel idea and made him long to leave this dangerous place so that they could be on their way.

He crept nearer the black enamel pipe and put his cold hands to it. Below he heard clearly the lid of the stove lifted aside as the coals were riddled.

"'Tis a cold bloody old night,' said a voice clearly.

The floorboard rocked as his foot shifted. It was loose and had obviously been shifted once to make way for the pipe. The cheap wood was warped and left a gap, handy enough no doubt for the mice which even now he thought he heard.

Finn unlaced his boots, so tired he would sleep in his clothes. His footwear would make ready missiles if the mice were trouble-some. He was about to get into bed when he heard Allan's voice.

He went back to the pipe; gingerly he raised the floorboard and put it to one side. The hole he had now made carried the sound as clearly as if the assembled Fenians were in the room with him.

The stove clanked again.

'For the second time,' said a voice with a strong Yankee accent, 'is Desmond's plan feasible?'

There was no reply. The voice renewed itself with some asperity, 'For God's sake, Allan, we don't ask for your blessing, just your opinion – '

'You was always knacky with dynamite,' put in another, gruffly.

' – is the thing possible? If our man takes cover behind the thick column that runs up the middle of the wall will he escape the full effects of the blast?'

'Crouching down. Taking exercise, tying his shoelace.'

Finn recognised the hard little voice of Desmond.

'There has to be a risk,' replied Allan.

'Damn the risk,' replied Desmond. 'Think of the effect of the thing, here in the heart of London. One bomb here is worth a score in Dublin.'

'Desmond,' put in the American voice, 'we are sure of our informant in the prison? He is in regular contact with Burke?'

'He has told us all we wish to know. Which yard Burke is exercised in – the one next to the road – at what time. It would be in the afternoon.'

'Our plan is to plant the explosive from the street alongside the prison wall. Two delivery men pushing a handcart will excite no interest – '

'And if the plan miscarries?' persisted Allan.

'Burke will be informed,' cut in Desmond's voice. 'The prison, being next to the street, is always having things thrown over the wall. If something goes wrong a child's white ball will be tossed over. Burke will be exercising at the time. When he sees the ball he will assume that we will attempt the next day.'

'It is a simple plan, Allan,' said the American voice. 'You yourself have always preached simplicity to us.'

There was a silence as if they waited Allan's reply. Finn, too, strained to catch it.

'Consider,' he said eventually, 'the amount of explosive needed to blow a hole in a prison wall. Consider the effect of that explosive detonated in a public thoroughfare in the broad afternoon. Explosives are no respecter of persons – '

'What is your meaning?' said Desmond.

'My meaning is that a score of innocent people will be killed.'

'This is a war, Captain Condent, or have you forgotten the fact? The idea of a war is to kill the enemy. They are going to hang innocent men in Manchester for the action you led. What are a score of English lives weighed in the balance of the millions of good Irishmen who have perished because of English indifference, cruelty, persecution?'

'Have we then become like them?'

Finn could detect the sadness in his voice.

'This is our turn,' said Desmond exultantly, 'the sword has been unsheathed. It cannot return to its scabbard until it has drunk blood.'

'Enough,' said the American with authority. 'There is another aspect of this we have not touched upon. I want you to take over this operation, Allan.'

There was a stunned silence.

'You are our best man with explosives and the coolest head in a crisis.'

'I am bound for France,' Allan's voice came in the barest whisper.

'Later. When it is over.'

'Finn – ' Finn shivered at the sound of his own name and drew back, as if they had seen him.

'Send him back where he came from – '

There was the sound of a chair scraping back.

'You would not refuse an order,' said the American, speaking slowly and with care. 'It carries too heavy a penalty.'

'What?' said Condent, incredulously. 'You would threaten me with death?'

'Understand this. No man is excused the consequences of the oath we swore. No matter how distinguished his service. We have the English by the throat – a blow of this nature delivered in the capital city would put them in a dead panic. You are the best man to lead. Lead you will – '

The chair fell back suddenly as if the occupant stood up abruptly. Footsteps walked across the floor –

'Allan.' The footsteps stopped. 'I am in deadly earnest.'

There was no reply; just the sound of a door closing.

Moments later the bedroom door opened. Finn was in the dusty bed, eyes closed, but conscious – too conscious – of eyes looking down on him. The interval stretched until he found the effort of keeping his face composed in its mask of sleep unbearable. A hand touched his hair gently.

'Allan,' Finn whispered. 'I heard it. All of it. Every word.'

And the dark hid the tears stealing on to the mouldy pillow.

The morning was squally; grey clouds raced over the rooftops while wind wrinkled the pools left in the road. Wheels splashed them over the shoes of passers-by, hurrying every way, clutching the flaps of their coats, holding tight to their hats. The wind roared; so did the traffic; so did the river, fierce and dark beneath the bridge where stood two figures oblivious to all that passed them by.

'I was proud. When I read what you did in Manchester I thought you had struck a blow for Ireland – '

A young woman covering a runny-nosed child with her shawl battled by them, bent against the thrust of the wind.

Finn followed her with his eyes. 'It could be her next. And the baby. The schoolteacher told me the Fenians fought for vengeance and I called him a liar. After what I heard last night I know he spoke the truth.'

Condent watched the hurrying clouds overhead and dropped his gaze to the racing waters beneath and spoke no word.

'He said – Mr Tipson said – unless you turn away, do not give back blow for blow, such matters will never end but get worse and worse.' Finn paused, fighting the beating of his heart, the tightness of his breath. He swallowed, 'Please do not do this thing.'

Condent looked down as if he had not heard the last words. 'He spoke the truth,' he said. 'I have come a long way from stories of Finn Mac Cool.'

He slid his hands into the sleeves of his coat, in the old way, and regarded the river. 'It were simpler to carry on than to go all the way back,' he said to himself.

'Take me to France like you said,' persisted Finn.

'If I do not obey they will kill me. Look at poor Dando.'

He put a hand on Finn's shoulder.

'It is finished. We must part.' The fingers gripped so tightly the limb ached for some moments afterwards. In Monkton he would see the small bruise each one made, each one a dark, hurt memory. 'Poor Finn, do not forget me. It is small chance ·you have had from life but I meant it otherwise. Forgive me.'

His face contracted, as if what he said cost him a great effort. Finn put up a hand to touch him.

'What is to forgive?'

'Only your life. When I am gone do not believe I meant to harm you. Do not believe I would do anything mean or evil. Dermot and your mother will care for you. Let us say good-bye now.'

The wind whipped at his dark head, at Finn's fair one; a

momentary light touched them. Then the clouds closed in once more.

The wind had been kept pretty much at it since Finn and Allan said good-bye on London Bridge a fortnight before. It had been in turn mighty and insinuating, throwing down towers, plaguing old men by their fires, rattling windows, whistling through keyholes. It cut like a knife and there was not a person, man, woman, or child, in the whole vast metropolis unaffected by it. But it had no power against devils.

Three devils walked behind a handcart in Clerkenwell. The wind chased through the spokes of the wheels, threw up the odd scrap of straw, worried at an old newspaper in the gutter, but could not disturb them. Their Mother was Murder; their names were homicide, fratricide, infanticide. They came following along behind two men pushing a handcart beneath the prison wall.

It was a good day for murder. Half-lit, as if the sun were afraid to rise to look on it. The shops lighted their lamps a good hour after noon and kept them burning in a lost effort to look cheery. Melancholy and drab at the best of times, the streets about the House of Correction were windswept and grey. The few feeble sprigs of holly hanging in the windows of the shops for Christmas knew the hopelessness of their position and drooped.

The handcart rattled by; below the ominous arm of the prison, past three boys playing jacks in its shelter, past the stall that sold hot potatoes, past the poor shops and the poor people who came out and went in, unaware of what was going by.

A brewer's dray was having an altercation with a two-horse omnibus. A policeman watched from the pavement in the manner of a referee, to see fair play. The handcart rattled on, disturbing the chickens who had wandered out from the area near by.

'Stop a bit.'

One of the men looked over his shoulder. As if he expected to see something. As if he knew the devils were at his elbow.

The other, whose ginger sidewhiskers showed plain beneath his bowler hat, clamped a cigar between his teeth and struck a match against the prison wall.

'For God's sake take care,' muttered the other.

87

The cigar smoker laughed, without unclenching his teeth.

'Lost your nerve, Captain Condent?'

Allan Condent glanced at the policeman. One policeman! He had sent two messages to the Governor of the prison that there would be an attempt and this was the response. Stupid, smug, blind!

'The English all over,' he said bitterly.

'The fuses, Captain.'

This street was his doom. If he had been arrested it would have been bad enough; but now there was no other way but to openly turn traitor. This was the end of all those whispered stories in the gloom of Condent Castle. Pushing death on a handcart.

'The fuses, if you please.'

'Tell those boys to go away, first.'

'Why not explain to them what we are about?' Desmond spat the words in a violent whisper. 'It's gone wrong once already because you couldn't get the fuses to light yesterday. Do you know what I think? I think you don't want this job to succeed. You're jealous because the plan isn't yours. Give me the fuses.'

'The policeman is looking.'

'He'll be wishing he didn't soon enough. Where are they?'

'I have not got them,' returned Condent calmly.

Desmond stared at him across the top of the barrel.

'You are correct, Desmond. I have been against this job from the start. I did not join the Brotherhood to kill innocent people. The fuses did not go off yesterday because I damped them. They will not go off today because I did not bring them with me. As of this moment I renounce the Brotherhood. I will leave you to push the cart home.'

He turned on his heel and began to walk away.

'Come back!' shouted Desmond after him, ignoring the policeman, who had indeed begun to take an interest in them, 'See this – traitor!'

He was brandishing something that looked like a firecracker.

'I brought a few squibs with me, just in case. Watch me now, Captain!'

He lit the touchpaper and when it glowed red dropped it into the top of the barrel.

'Hey boys!' cried Desmond as he broke into a run. 'Do you like fireworks?'

The children broke off from their game to stare.

The policeman had begun to walk across to the barrel as Desmond drew his revolver and shot at Condent.

The world turned white.

Allan Condent was not dead. He got to his feet, staggering a little. The air was filled with choking dust, something was on fire, somewhere a baby was crying.

Where the wall had been gaped a huge, jagged hole revealing the prison yard. It was empty. So they had taken some notice after all. Today the prisoners had not been exercised. It had all been a huge waste of time. He began to laugh.

Along that stretch of death they were the only human sounds: the baby crying, the man laughing.

CHAPTER TWELVE
The Fugitive

The time of the new baby was at hand. Dermot fretted and chafed and his company became unbearable.

Finn chose to sit with Marcus in the mill. Work was over for the day, the wheel was silent, the bins were full. Dark had come on and they sat by the light of the mill lantern while the mill cats stretched and went to look for mice, and Sam the dog snored at their feet. Neither of them were in any hurry to return to the houses but sat in silence, listening to the owl hooting two fields away.

'Cissie was pleased when you come back, I'll lay,' murmured Marcus at length.

Finn's re-appearance had not caused much comment as Dermot had been shrewd enough to say little about his absence except in terms of a short holiday.

'She wasn't pleased.' She had behaved most strangely.

'Ar? So that explains why you've been so drear and moidery since you come back.' Marcus whistled softly.

'She said she hadn't missed me at all. She had been glad I had gone away – that's what she said. But it isn't Cissie I'm thinking of, I know she still likes me. At least, I think she does . . .'

'But if it 'tidn't love that's eating you then what is it?'

'Nothing, Marcus.' Then later, 'What is all this news they are talking of – an explosion in London?'

'Tiddle taddle. It don't signify what the folks in London gets up to, 'tis all nonsense. Best left alone – '

Sam put his head up, ears pricked, tail thumping on the floor. The door was thrust open and Dermot poked his head around it.

'Go to Grammer Creech's,' he said to Finn. 'Tell her it has started – '

He was gone clattering back to the house.

'The baby, you great calf,' said Marcus. 'The old lady will help it

to come. Get you moving – 'tis the hardest work your mother will
have for many a long day. She needs all the assistance she can get.
Off you go now.'

Finn had never got beyond the door of Cissie's cottage before.
The old woman busied herself, getting her things together, throwing the odd remark to Cissie who sat by the fire primly with her
book.

'You may hop from one leg to t'other if you will,' she observed to
the boy, 'but I'm an old body and can't hurry. Besides the baby will
not be coming for a while yet.'

The smell he always associated with Cissie was overwhelming.
Bunches of herbs hung upside down from the beams, like bats, and
in the window there were more. A pot steamed gently, giving off an
odour he had never encountered before, sharp and green.

''Tis a well-made youth,' exclaimed Grannie, taking down one
of the bunches and securing them in her purse with a snap.

'Grannie – ' Cissie laid by her book.

'Why so coy, maid? You have spoken of 'en often enough.'

Finn blushed to his hair; the gloom hid his shame and his
pleasure.

'No maid, you may shake your curly locks at I, but my own mother
was wedded and bedded when she was your own age.'

She brought the shawl close about her head, her gnarled fingers
snapping at her throat, looking at Finn with a wicked gleam.

'Give us thy hand – left hand, left hand.' Her own hand was cold.
'Thin old blood,' she said by way of explanation.

She studied his palm closely, eyes an inch or two from his hand.
He had only time to exchange a glance with Cissie, who sat in her
corner, cheeks aglow.

'A good palm,' she said. 'A catch for any maid. You will be a rich
man one day,' she giggled. 'The maid has more sense than I gave
her credit for. But let us go now and see what comfort we may bring
to your mother.'

At the mill he was left by the fire with Sam for company. Marcus
had gone home.

Upstairs were footsteps, the creaking of the old brass bed, once
– to his unease – a sharp cry of pain. Voices murmuring, more steps;
Grannie Creech's shuffle back and forth across the floor, Dermot

walking up and down the passageway outside. In the yard the gate was banging in the wind. Finn put on more wood and watched the sparks fly away up into the darkness of the chimney.

There had been gossip all day about an explosion in London. Many dead, 'they Irish' at the bottom of it, no more details to be had. Marcus had meant kindness when he had refused to discuss it but Finn longed to hear every detail, to talk instead of thinking.

He picked up the lamp and walked to the window. Upstairs there came another cry. He shivered. Tonight he was full of dread; he thought of those who were dead, of Vellew and Dando and wondered about those who were living, all trapped by some inexplicable means, in the same web. He held up his lantern to the night. The river went by, brawling in the gloom; the light from the lamp threw the pattern of the window on to the water, all the way to the other bank.

He went back to the inner door. Dermot was sitting in the gloom of the passageway.

'Go you out and shut the gate,' he said. 'I do not want to be hearing it when she's in pain.'

Finn hurried across the yard, his light dancing above the ground like the soul of some poor infant on Hallowe'en. He had to put it down to fasten the gate –

'Finn, is that you there?'

The whisper came from the corner of the barn and the wall where shadows hung the thickest.

'Yes – '

'Is it safe?' like a sigh.

'Grannie Creech is here,' Finn strained forward and addressed the darkest part of the shadows. 'The baby is coming.'

'God forgive me, I had forgot. I'll go into the barn. Tell Dermot I'm here.'

Dermot was boiling a big pan of water on the kitchen range when he got back. He left it to its own devices and came to the barn at once. Allan Condent sat among the straw. By the lamplight his eyes glittered; his skin was like paper, his hair like soot, damp with perspiration clinging to his brow. His smile flickered briefly.

'I come at a bad time. How is it, Dermot?'

Dermot's hands attempted a gesture, gave up. 'The old baby is lying the wrong way. And you?'

'They are watching all the main ports. I am on my way to Porlock where I may slip away without notice. I need to rest here – only for an hour. Go back to Mary – '

'She will not have me near her. It went badly with you? The village has been full of talk.'

'Badly,' Allan grimaced. 'Every hand is against me now. If I escape from Ireland I will go to America. I will write from there.'

'I do not understand – '

'You refused to obey?' Finn broke in, eyes alight. 'You would not do it?'

Dermot looked from one to the other.

Finn's face was suffused with pride. A great weight had shifted; his mind was clear and sharp. He put a hand on Allan's arm.

'I am glad.'

Allan's lips twisted. 'Then you are the only one. It will be a bullet from the rest of them – '

'You have left them?' put in Dermot.

'And betrayed them to the English.'

Dermot was thunderstruck.

'It was the only thing he could do,' explained Finn. 'And even then it did not stop the killing.' He saw it all at once, with startling clarity.

'Then to go to Ireland is madness,' said Dermot staring.

Allan sighed, a tired man. 'I will be there only long enough to arrange a passage to America. The English are looking for me, too. I cannot stay here.'

'At least stay the night.'

'You should be with Mary. Your own troubles outweigh mine at this moment. I will be over the moor and on the way to Porlock within the hour.'

'I shall come with you,' said Finn firmly. 'You are tired and might need help. A companion shortens any walk – '

'No – '

'Yes. There is no danger at this time of night.'

Dermot scratched his beard, the hairs on his forearm glinting golden in the light. 'Take a lantern, Finn. Take also the knapsack that hangs behind the door and fill it with bread and cheese, some apples, too, and a bottle of water to drink – '

'Go back to Mary now,' said Allan.

'Forgive me, my old friend, but I am as nervous as a girl tonight. If I could just listen at her door . . .'

Finn had already slipped out.

'Dermot – ' the door was ajar and Dermot the other side of it, ' – if you love me do not tell her anything now. I will write when I am able.'

'Yes, write all about it,' said Dermot, his mind already with his wife. 'God go with you.'

Finn led the way. They slipped silent through the village and up the hill where there was no light and the blackness immense. They heard the wind on the other side of the valley but here were protected from it. Once or twice a fox barked and once they stood stock still as something heavy crashed away from them among the undergrowth.

'Deer,' Finn whispered.

There were no stars to guide them; even the tall oaks at either hand had been swallowed by the night. It was a good night for a fugitive.

Allan laughed softly, the same thought in his mind. 'Do you remember the book you were reading that first night?'

'*Old Mortality* – and you asked me if helping someone to escape was the sort of tale I admired. But this isn't like a book, is it?'

'It never is,' replied Allan grimly.

At the top of the hill the wind hit, going deep into their insides like draughts of cold water. The path was no more than a deer track but the night was a shade lighter.

'Mask the lantern,' ordered Allan. 'Walk in front.'

The boy was fresher than the man and paused several times for him to catch up. Perhaps he had walked too far already; certainly at the mill he had looked done in.

'Slow but steady,' muttered Allan ruefully. 'My legs have lost their strength.'

'Are you unwell?'

'I am . . . tired.'

They spoke no more. The heather whistled a little, a few drops of rain spattered coldly on their faces, but they were alone. The night belonged to them. Finn began to half run; fleet as a deer, he thought, like Finn Mac Cool. He began to enjoy the sense of freedom that came with the open moor and imagined himself leading a silent raiding party. For he was lighthearted at the thought that Allan had not obeyed orders; had refused to shed innocent blood. It mattered to him more than he could say.

He stopped. The gap for Allan to come up was more than ever. He must have walked miles to get to Monkton; he was done in. Twice he thought he saw something, twice the night deceived him. All around the darkness was implacable; he drew back the cover of the light but its glare illumined only a few paltry yards and made the rest blacker than ever. Slowly he began to retrace his steps; he could hear no following footsteps. He swung the lantern this way and that as he walked and wondered, to no purpose, if anyone saw the light blinking out at sea.

His foot stumbled against something soft. He lost balance and trod on Allan's outflung hand before righting himself. He was lying face downward on the path, limbs outstretched, like a man washed up by a silent black sea.

Finn set down his light and attempted to turn the heavy body. His hand came away wet. He thought Allan was lying in a puddle until he saw, by the lamp's yellow glow, the staining on his fingers.

'Desmond,' said Allan, with a groan. The rest of what he said was lost in a muffled mutter before his head lifted slightly. He paused and the breath rattled hoarsely in his throat, 'Finn, is that you?'

'You are bleeding,' said Finn wondering.

'I am glad you were proud,' said Allan, or at least that is what it sounded like as his head was muffled by his arm once more. He laughed softly, 'I cannot decide whether it is Desmond's bullet or part of the prison wall that is lodged in me. I stopped the bleeding for a time but it has burst out again . . .'

'Can you walk at all?'

He did not seem to hear. 'How cold it is.'

'We have not come so far. If you can walk we might go back to the mill.'

95

'No – ' Allan's hand sought Finn's. 'You must understand Finn. I cannot go there, tonight of all nights.'

'Because of the baby?' asked Finn, with surprise.

'Yes. I have interfered too much in their lives. Besides, I bring danger with me. Where are we?'

As if in reply a break in the clouds revealed the squat shape of the tower above the dark line of the trees.

'Condent's Folly,' he laughed once more, as his face contracted with a spasm of pain, 'Condent's Folly – what could be more fitting?'

'Do not laugh like that – ' said Finn desperately. There was a note in it of abandon, of a man who was preparing to let go of his life.

'Take me there. It is out of the wind at least.'

It was less than half a mile away, though a fit man could have walked four good miles in the time they took. Once he was up, Condent became more composed, alternately limping and resting on Finn; telling him – between gasps for breath – how twice he had betrayed the Fenians to the governor of the prison, how he had not brought the fuses, but how, in the end, he had failed.

'Many casualties,' he said. 'You cannot conceive . . .' Here he broke off, as if he saw the scene before him once more in the staring blackness of the night. 'Let us walk,' he said abruptly.

The bleeding was steady, seeping through his clothes, staining the branches that brushed him, yet not dripping on the ground. He had been able, he told Finn, to roughly bandage his wound at the house of Fenian sympathisers near the prison. It had not seemed so bad then. He had continued at once, travelling alone most of the way on the train. He was determined to flee the country.

They climbed down from the ridge they had gained, through meadows heavy with moisture, then once more upward to the hill on which the Folly stood. Built a hundred years before, by a wealthy Condent, for no other purpose than to introduce a picturesque note into the scenery and provide work for the villagers in winter, it now was to provide a haven for his hunted descendant.

'I will make a bit of a fire where no one will see it,' said Finn encouragingly.

They were gasping for breath with their backs to its solid sand-stone walls. Above, the night was encircled by the hollow coronet of the tower; blackness pressed in through the empty gothic arches of the windows; bats flitted to and fro like small birds in a yew tree. The sturdy wall shut off the wind, near the buttresses the ground was sandy and dry.

'You must eat.' Finn offered him broken bread and cheese. 'Here, there is water in this bottle and in this something stronger – Dermot gave it to me before I came away – it will warm you.'

Allan obeyed like a child. While he was eating Finn set about gathering kindling and bigger lumps of wood of which there was no shortage. He split the logs by smashing them against the sharp buttress of the wall and tossed them on the blaze as the flames took.

Although the glow revealed Allan's face to be haggard and drawn, the improvement in his manner was striking. Food and drink had put new heart in him.

'I cannot tell you how grateful I am to you, Finn,' he said. 'But you must go home now.' He corked the dark bottle and laid it by him. 'You have gathered enough wood to see me through the night. I will sleep and in the morning try for Porlock once more.'

'I will come.'

'In daytime there will be much danger. Go home.'

As the kitchen door closed behind him he became conscious of something new; a hush, a stillness in the house. Then he heard heavy footsteps across the floor and the deep muttering of Dermot's voice; as if in response came a sound that transfixed him.

He stood there with his hands still on the latch and the hot tears burning down his cheeks. He could not tell why he wept: for all of them, for Allan, for himself, for the new baby who was crying with him.

CHAPTER THIRTEEN
Some Advice

For an interval Tipson's pen whispered soothingly across the paper, leaving behind a neat and elegant line of words. 'Some thoughts on Etruscan Tombs.' He was seated among the remains of his breakfast, his morning cup of coffee resting on a copy of Milton's *Paradise Lost*. He enjoyed this quiet hour before school, but more and more his pupils elbowed their way in among his finer thoughts. Take the boy Finn Hagan, for the most part a bright and attentive lad, he had for the past two days been pale, withdrawn, nervous. Was the boy ill? Or was there something going on at home. The new baby?

Tipson laid down his pen with a sigh. It was no use, Etruscan tombs must wait; and after all, they had waited long enough as it was.

His housekeeper came in and cleared away; a large, slow-moving woman, somewhat in awe of her master and all his book learning.

As luck would have it, the subject of his ruminations came by his window. First Tipson thought Finn was come early to school, then there was ringing of the doorbell.

'Well, sir,' he creaked around in his chair and regarded Finn through narrowed eyes. 'What may I do for you?'

He was as pale as ever and as restless, he shifted from one foot to the other, at a loss as to how to begin. Tipson invited him to sit down and requested the housekeeper to bring the boy a hot cup of tea.

'You are not unwell?' he asked kindly. 'Mother and baby in the best of health?'

No, it was not that.

The silence lengthened and Tipson's clock ticked thoughtfully to itself from the corner.

'Yes, there is a good view from this window. As the sun rises it picks out the tower in the most splendid way. It is a curious thing but I like it – there is a lot to be said for folly.'

Finn flushed guiltily and tore his gaze away from the tower. 'I want to read about the explosion in Clerkenwell,' he said abruptly.

Two days had passed since he had left Allan up there. Dermot had taken over since that night. Allan was not well enough to move: Dermot was going to see Lady Condent today to solicit her aid for her son.

Without a word Tipson struggled to his feet and began to rummage among his papers.

'You said before how the Irish have suffered at the hands of the English, how millions died in the Hunger. Wouldn't you say it was fair, served them right because the Irish fight back?' Finn felt he was struggling for the words.

'A just war?' Tipson looked up sharply. 'Because of what the British did to them, they are justified in what they do to the British. Is that what you mean?'

Finn said nothing. The teacher took his silence for agreement.

'Are the dead and mutilated in Clerkenwell any less dead or mutilated because of what the British did in Ireland?'

Tipson found the journal he was looking for but did not give it over immediately.

'Do you remember yesterday afternoon when I caught Barty Purvis tormenting the school cat? His excuse was that Reuben Cooper did it first. Do you remember what my reply was?'

Finn shook his head.

'Well, my reply was what it always is when that excuse is offered – "Never mind what Reuben Cooper did, *you* knew it was wrong". Will God – or whoever it is who judges mankind – have any sympathy with the Irish if they offer the excuse that the British did it first?'

Finn kept silence.

'Are men swine that follow one another over the precipice?'

Tipson limped back to the table. 'The older generations have paddled their hands in blood,' he said more gently. 'Our only hope lies in the people of your generation. Where will it all end if the thinking does not change?'

He gave the newspaper to the boy and observed him as he read, noting with attention the tightening of his mouth, the intensity of his eyes, as each detail was taken in.

"Houses windowless, cracked brickwork, shaken chimneys . . . devastation beyond belief . . . the mangling of innocent women and children . . . forty dead . . ." the correspondent had spared no detail in his graphic description and the phrases fell like a cold rain over the poor, huddled figure up there in the tower.

'The man they wanted to free is still in captivity,' observed Tipson drily.

'I know,' said Finn, putting the newspaper down. 'They had been warned and changed the exercise times.'

He may have read that very fact in the account he had just put away, but something in his manner of saying it caused the schoolteacher to regard him thoughtfully, a dim, wild suspicion forming itself in the background.

Finn rubbed his eyes as if they were tired. 'Imagine a man . . .'

Tipson continued to regard him steadily.

'You were kind to me before – when you talked to me and played Carrickfergus. You helped me then, and I have thought of what you said to me often. You seemed so sure you knew what was right. And I know you will treat me in all confidence.'

'Very well.'

'Imagine a man – '

'I do not care for hypothetical cases. What man – your father?'

'Someone I met . . . when I was away.'

Tipson nodded. Come to think of it there had been a change since he had returned from his holiday.

'A man involved in this,' Finn touched the paper, 'who did not want it to happen. Who informed not once but twice, who did all he could to prevent it, but who was there – ' Finn paused. 'Would such a man be a murderer?'

'In whose eyes?'

To Tipson it was scarcely credible that national events could reach in and touch him here, safe in his schoolmaster's house in Somerset. He kept his tone steady and did not betray the rising sense of unreality he was feeling.

'You spoke of God just now.'

'I am not God,' replied the teacher sharply.

'But you are a good man,' said Finn simply.

Tipson sighed, 'If there were such a man and he truly felt as you describe and behaved in the way you describe then I think . . .' his voice trailed away as he remembered the interest Finn displayed in the Manchester episode. Was this boy involved – even on the fringes – of both events? 'I think he would be tired of his life at this moment. But a murderer, no. I think also that the law will hunt him down with the utmost severity and his pleas will carry little weight in an English court. I think, Finn, and I speak as your true friend here, that if you truly know such a person then you would be best advised to have no more to do with him. This is not a game you are playing.'

He sank back in his chair.

'It makes all my talk of a moment ago seem like so many empty and overblown words,' he said. He felt helpless. 'Tell your father of what I have said.'

When Finn had gone Tipson remained at the table for some moments. At length he stirred, realising that his eye had rested for some time on the open page of his journal and his thoughts on Etruscan tombs. He snapped the volume shut and threw it away from him in disgust. All at once it seemed that his life had been wasted on futile thoughts; that his deeds had all been futile things.

CHAPTER FOURTEEN
Lady Condent

The sun broke through the open crown of Condent's Folly striking the sleeper across the face. His head shifted: in his dreams he had been wandering the dark castle of his boyhood, trying doors that would not open. Now, with a blaze of glory, he had found the right door and his sleeping face smiled.

Into the small patch of dry earth walked a lady. Her wisps of grey hair become like spiders' webs, the buckles of her shoes dim with dust. She was not alone, but her companion lingered in the shadows.

The winter sun, and there was no warmth in it, lighted on the crown of her head, cruelly exposing the pink scalp beneath the wispy hair. There was little warmth in the lady either; she bent her head and studied the sleeper. His face, whose skin seemed already dead, the eyes like two dark bruises; had they dumped a pile of old clothes by the roadside to be splashed by every passing vehicle, the effect would have been much the same. She did not bend to rearrange his coat or to touch him but remained immobile, only her glance, distant and misty, like the sun, passing over his body.

He was awake, looking up at her. Something welled up in his eyes, like blood from a wound, then died away. 'I was dreaming,' he said.

'Dermot Hagan said I should find you here.' Lady Condent's fingers twitched at the black stuff of her skirt. 'He put your life in my hands.'

'It is but poor coin, I fancy,' returned her son, in a whisper that haunted her old neglected heart. 'Death is with me dealing . . .'

She remained steady and unbending, but her hand began to crush at the skirt with agitation. She glanced, as if for help, to the shadows. 'A doctor,' she faltered. 'You are wounded.'

102

'Dermot thinks a son should say good-bye to his mother.' There was a grating edge to his voice. 'Dermot was always the one to do the decent thing. He would have made a better son than I.'

'Allan . . .'

'Good-bye, mother.'

'Not a word, not a line of writing in all these years . . .'

From where he lay her head was encircled by the rim of the tower; her old face like a martyr's. 'Why did you turn your back on me?'

'Enough,' he said, turning away.

'This talk of dying – '

'There is something in my gut making an end of me,' he replied harshly, facing the wall.

Then she knelt. Her hand strayed to his face, then hesitated. 'A doctor . . .'

'Would make me well only for them to hang me. I was one of those at Clerkenwell.'

Despite herself, she shot another nervous glance to the shadows.

'Who is there?' he demanded.

'No one . . . only my chaplain, Mister Pinecoffin . . . I could not have made the journey through the passage unassisted.'

'He is not to be trusted. Though I am past caring – '

'To end here – '

'This is Condent's Folly,' he said bitterly. 'It is where I belong.'

Her eyes glittered. 'To be remembered as a – ' She could not name the word.

'A murderer. Yes. A traitor too . . . double traitor.'

Allan Condent ground his teeth together. 'Mother, why did you not love me when you had the chance? There is nothing you can do for me now. You have come too late.'

The old lady's face opened foolishly; the eyes and the mouth wide, as if he had struck at her heart.

The gloom of the passage suited Septimus Pinecoffin on the return journey; his mood, his heart, his face. The light kept him in shadow as he held the lamp aloft with one hand, guided the lady with the other.

'There is that recumbent timber,' he muttered. 'Looking more like a dead man than ever.'

He had tripped over it on the way out, spoiling his trousers, though the trip, he reflected, the trip as a whole was likely to cost him more than a pair of black serge unmentionables. The prodigal son had returned.

Vellew and – what was the mountebank actor's name? – Dando, had been right all along. Allan Condent was alive and up to his ears in monkey business. And Lady Condent, the goose that laid the golden eggs, was going soft on him.

Pinecoffin was shaken. He didn't want his pitch queered at this particular moment by the prodigal son. He didn't like it; neither would Sammle Wentworth like it. Not Sam. No more gravy for Sam. No more nights on the town with a flash gal on each knee.

You could have knocked him down with a feather when the old lady had come to their morning Bible reading waving a great iron key.

'No psalms today,' she had said. 'I wish you to accompany me.'

All them psalms, sung through the nose every day for six months, all them bleeding psalms thrown away after a two minute interview with a bundle of rags.

'It is a secret few are privy to,' she had said. She took him to a cellar where a false half-barrel was moved aside to reveal a small wooden door. 'My ancestor had a picturesque imagination. He loved secret passages, ruins, towers.'

'It is a passage to the Folly?' enquired Pinecoffin faintly. 'My dear lady, is it safe?'

'It has not been used for many years. I little thought I would ever use it, but I must go to the tower as secretly as possible.'

The journey took almost half an hour. She had not told him what they were to see; Pinecoffin's hands grew quite sweaty with anticipation. He couldn't put away the childish conviction that she was going to show him some treasure, or something of that nature. He was thinking of what form it might take – gold, jewels, old coins – when he fell flat on his face, tripping over the timber.

Some treasure; the prodigal son trying to die before he was hanged.

'Madam,' he said, as they emerged into the comparative light of the cellar, 'I feel I must warn you – '

She turned her sharp face to him; he quailed inwardly but went on in his most impressive manner. 'This ingrate must not be aided. Leave him to those who call themselves his friends. Woe to him who bites the hand that fed him!'

Not impressive enough. Desperately he tried again. 'If you help him you lay yourself open to the full penalty of the law.'

The words fell away from him, overblown and rotten, petals from a flower whose short day is done.

She looked at him as if seeing him for the first time. He felt strangely naked in the cold air of the cellar.

'You always told me he was dead,' he faltered.

Her mind had been running along the same old story. 'I had a son that was dead,' she said with a toss of her grey head. 'But now he has come back to life. I had a son that was lost and now he is found.'

'The Master will gather up the good grain into his barn.' It was one last desperate attempt to impose himself. 'But the chaff will be consumed by the everlasting fire.'

She was not even listening. 'This must be spoken of to no one,' she said curtly, turning away without waiting for him to finish. His power over her was gone. A vain, self-deluding woman, she had stumbled over something so real and jagged it had torn through the tissue of false religiosity he had wrapped her in.

Pinecoffin watched her go up the stone steps, without attempting to follow, tears of rage stinging his eyes.

CHAPTER FIFTEEN
Betrayal

Each time he looked out of the window the tower on the horizon seemed to expand. As if it was a great belly; great pregnant belly ready to burst.

He was sitting in Vellew's business parlour, a glass of opium in his hand. His toothache was back. Have a sleep in a moment when he'd finished considering what to do. No psalms this morning, Lady Condent had sent a message begging to be excused.

'Ho – ' he said aloud, 'she isn't the only one who can send messages.'

He chuckled and attempted – without success – to stare the tower out of countenance and repeated, 'Not the only one who can send messages, my fine lad.'

The tower, or what it sheltered, was his doom. Lady Condent was finished with him. No more readies for the little fatherless and motherless darlings in Wapping. Sammle Wentworth wouldn't like it. He had come to enjoy living in the country with regular trips to town. What a life; the idle rich, that's what he had been.

His head had begun to nod forward on to his chest when he was disturbed by the maid. He beamed and stirred himself; fine armful that girl was. Old Sammle would like to gather her charms in his arms. But no, that wouldn't do – he wasn't Sammle Wentworth, he was Septimus Pinecoffin. Holy Joe Pinecoffin.

'Yes, my dear?' he said unctuously.

She favoured him with a pout that made the backs of his legs tingle.

'Gentleman ... odd sort of gentleman, asking for you on particular business.'

Pinecoffin stiffened and straightened himself. Even half drunk, he looked immaculate. 'Military sort of man?' he enquired faintly. 'I might be expecting word from a military man.'

'Greetings, dear brother, in this heathen land of the Hittite and the Amorite – '

Pinecoffin blinked in astonishment. The maid curtseyed and fled without a further word.

'This dwelling of Belial and Beelzebub – '

Perhaps the opium was already working. But no, here he was at Vellew's desk, leather top scratched and scarred; he couldn't dream a desk like that.

'Glenlivet, Angus.' The visitor presented a blunt hand, like a spade, and with it a strong odour of tobacco and spirits. There was too much of him to take in at once; ginger sidewhiskers, bloodshot eyes, potatoey nose.

'I don't know you,' Pinecoffin said rudely.

'Glenlivet, Angus. Scotch. Scots wae hae.' Mister Glenlivet also wore a ginger wig, slightly askew.

'Please,' Pinecoffin pressed his hand to his temple, 'don't go on so. Stop talking like a telegraph machine. What can I do for you, Mr . . . er – '

'Glenlivet. But did I not understand you were a gentleman of the cloth, Mr Pinecoffin?' A burring roll on the 'r's certified the strange visitor's Scots antecedents.

'Private,' said Pinecoffin firmly. 'I am Lady Condent's private chaplain. I make no claim to belong to any of the established churches.'

As it was plain he was not going to be invited to sit down, Mr Glenlivet perched himself on the edge of the desk and loomed forward blocking off the light.

'Are we alone?'

'Unless there's someone under the desk.'

'Very humorous.' The smile grew even more menacing. Pinecoffin closed his eyes. When he opened them Glenlivet was still looming over him.

'Samuel Wentworth,' said Glenlivet.

He dropped the name idly, as a man might drop a stone in a pool. There was an interval while its ripples spread through the room. Pinecoffin rose to his feet and crossed to the door in case the maid was listening. Getting to his feet made him dizzy.

'Samuel Wentworth,' repeated Glenlivet.

Some reply seemed to be called for. 'I do know a gentleman of that name,' admitted Pinecoffin cautiously.

He held on to the doorknob for support. There were black hairs poking from underneath Glenlivet's ginger wig but somehow it did not seem the time to mention this interesting fact.

'I'm not an old lady,' said Glenlivet. 'Ye'll have to do a wee bit better than that. Do you remember George Dando?'

Pinecoffin nodded.

'The spy,' said Glenlivet. 'George and myself have done business together and one night, over a glass or two, he told me the whole tale. He came here when he was following Allan Condent, didn't he? He had a long talk with the lady of the house. She spoke, George said, at damnable length about some orphanage in Wapping which she had founded with your help. Every night the bairns assemble by her portrait and pray for her and give thanks for her munificence. Or so she said. Her Cause, she called it. A prosy lady.'

Pinecofin remained where he was. Glenlivet perched on the desk like a vulture; the tower listened to all that passed and chuckled.

'The same Dando,' resumed Glenlivet, 'quite by chance happened to be passing The Royal Parks Hotel in Victoria one day. Who should be coming out but Mr Septimus Pinecoffin, with the doorman bowing and scraping, showing him to his carriage as if he was the Duke of Devonshire. You cut him dead – a bad mistake, my friend, for George was always on the I-spy. He asked the doorman for your name and was told that you were calling yourself Samuel Wentworth. As soon as he was able he went to Wapping to poke about on his own account. After several hours he was prepared to take his oath. No orphanage.'

Glenlivet ran his nail the length of the desk splitting the leather completely. 'No orphanage. No cause. The good lady had been providing funds for an institution that has no existence outside her own pious mind. The question must be put – where are said funds, who's had them?'

108

'Samuel Wentworth is a dear friend ...' faltered Pinecoffin. 'Common error ... the resemblance ...'

'It's time to put an end to Samuel Wentworth, my friend. He spends too much money. There's just the two of us in it now.'

'George Dando – '

'Dead,' murmured Glenlivet, touching his hat respectfully. 'In an alley. "As ye sow so will ye reap".'

Pinecoffin gaped and shrank away.

'Who killed him? I'll tell ye a wee secret. It was myself.' Glenlivet lifted an imaginary dagger. 'In, out. In, out. Shake it all about.'

There was a chair by the door. Pinecoffin dropped into it and passed a hand over his eyes. The chair was of oak, he could see the grain of the wood with utter clarity. Everything else was puddled.

'Who the devil are you?'

'I'm just a dishonest, thieving, murdering sort of chap. There's no need to be afraid,' said Glenlivet kindly. He came and put a hand on Pinecoffin's shoulder. 'You'd be surprised how often people kill people in my line of work. And after all, the world should be a better place with one less villain in it – though George did have a beautiful speaking voice. Not to mention one less to go shares with. We are partners now – have you no a wee dram to cement our partnership?'

Pinecoffin fetched the glasses and they drank a glass of wine together. Pinecoffin fearfully, Glenlivet with great enjoyment, holding his glass up to the light and smacking his lips when it was finished.

'I'll see you all right, Septimus,' he said. 'Have no fears wi' me. Finish up your drink. Or is it because you already have a drink taken that you're so slow?'

'You want to put an end to Samuel.' Pinecoffin withdrew his hand from underneath Glenlivet's.

'No–o.' Glenlivet poured another glass and pushed it into Pinecoffin's hand. 'Not now I see how things are between you both. Septimus in the country and Samuel in the town, is it? Sam needn't be a bother to us.' He patted Pinecoffin's hand once more and gestured towards the ledgers that lined the walls,

Vellew's accounts, 'No one could blame you for having a wee bit of money out of them. All that money, this great big house, one old woman with no use for any of it. Does she have a steward?'

The warmth of his tone engulfed Pinecoffin like a blanket. Out of the window the tower had shrunk so small he seemed to be viewing it through the wrong end of a telescope. This pleased him. He took more wine.

'I do everything now. Vellew used to . . .'

'Vellew?'

'The estate manager. This was his office. He cheated her too. Little Vellew, the faithful steward, been doing it for years and years. I found him out.'

'Oh, but you're the sharp one, Septimus. Try putting anything over on you, oh no.' He patted Pinecoffin's hand in a fatherly way.

Pinecoffin giggled; he was beginning to like Glenlivet.

'So Lady Condent sacked him?'

'No, he wasn't sacked.' Pinecoffin paused for breath and hiccuped. 'I killed him.'

Glenlivet chuckled admiringly and dug Pinecoffin in the ribs. 'You dog,' he said. 'That's capital, you killed him. Here, your glass is empty, let me . . . so.' He waved his imaginary knife, 'In, out. In, out, shake it all about – did you? No, it wasn't the knife? Poison? No, well tell me in your own way. I think I'll have a drop while I listen. Here, let me fill up your glass once more. Talking is thirsty work.'

Pinecoffin flung his legs out before him, and sat back expansively, revelling in the admiring attention he was being given.

'Lady Condent invited me to look at the books – to see if there were any more funds for the Cause. He was a most honest thief; he would sell a piece of woodland for three hundred pounds, let us say, and enter the bill of sale at that price. Yet two or three pages further on the same transaction would be entered under the column marked "Income" at two hundred and seventy five. The odd twenty five pounds he kept for himself.'

'That's no very subtle,' observed Glenlivet.

'Childish.' Pinecoffin leaned forward, somewhat too abruptly, and hiccuped gravely. 'A child could have spotted it. But of course no one ever checked the books. Lady Condent trusted him implicitily, implicital – she trusted him.'

Pinecoffin sat back, tapped his nose with his finger, and winked, ''Course, I didn't split, oh no.'

'Oh, no,' agreed Glenlivet.

'Once I told him I had tumbled his little game he was in my pocket. He could be useful to me. She – ' he gestured to the ceiling, as if Lady Condent was in the room above, 'she told me her son Allan was dead, yet Vellew let drop he lived. Then there was the Irish family at the mill. Where did Allan Condent disappear?'

'Ireland.'

'Of course. And here is Vellew bringing in an Irish family, pushing the boy, Finn Hagan, on Lady Condent as if there was something special about him, the brat. I made Vellew give them notice.'

'And did he?' enquired Glenlivet, peering at Pinecoffin through narrowed eyes.

'Had to. Else I would have gone to milady with the news. But – ' Pinecoffin frowned, 'the little man was loyal. One night he came to me – he'd been drinking – and as good as told me to go to the devil. He was going to tell them they could stay. Said he'd sworn to be loyal to Master Allan. He marched off to do it too, even though it was past midnight. I followed through the village and caught up with him by the river. It was a wild night and the river was in flood. I argued, swore at him, threatened him. In the end he tried to hit me. I pushed him away. Splash! He was gone before I could recover myself.'

Pinecoffin didn't know whether to grin or not, Glenlivet was looking at him in such a peculiar manner.

'Upon the whole, I rather think I killed him. I ran home and hid, but no one ever suspected me. The joke of it was that they all thought the miller, Dermot Hagan, did it. But I'm glad you've come, here – ' he crooked his finger and Glenlivet bent close. 'Equal shares, right? You see, there might be a slight difficulty until I can bring Lady Condent round again.'

He pointed to the tower. 'Allan Condent is here.'

'Here?' Glenlivet looked around sharply.

'There. The tower, he's wounded. Don't worry, don't worry.' It was his turn to pat Glenlivet's hand reassuringly. 'I've taken care of all that. At this moment the soldiers are marching down to Monkton to take him.'

Glenlivet took Pinecoffin by the throat and shook him. 'What the devil do you mean?' he growled. 'Speak up, or I'll slit your nose you yellow-bellied canting hypocrite. What do you mean?'

Pinecoffin's eyes bulged. He tried to speak but no sound came forth; his tongue worked frantically. Glenlivet eased his hold slightly.

'You're choking me!'

'Yes, my wee man. Now speak up if you wish to improve the quality of your breathing. What were you saying about soldiers?'

'I sent a message ... sent a message to the garrison in Taunton. Told them one of the Clerkenwell bombers was in hiding in Condent's Folly! That's who I thought you were at first!'

Glenlivet shoved him back into his chair and glowered down at him.

'You'd even betray her son,' he said.

'If he comes back it'll be the end of the Cause,' said Pinecoffin sulkily, settling his collar and feeling his neck tenderly. 'It'll be no use you coming round then. Anyhow, who asked you to push in? I was getting on all right before you came.'

Glenlivet poked a blunt finger at him. 'I am in. That's all that need concern you. One word from you about me and I will come back here and finish you. You understand me, my bonnie wee man?'

Pinecoffin nodded, still sulky. He shrank away from the upraised finger.

'I'm away,' said Glenlivet. 'To see how I can mend this business.'

CHAPTER SIXTEEN
Flight

The wound was a rat gnawing at his vitals; sharp teeth in his insides. His cries swirled among the bare walls while birds flew in through the empty windows and fluttered up to a sky the colour of a winter sea.

The earth floor made a cold bed. Propping himself on his elbow he could see, through a gap in the crumbling wall, fields that spread scrubbily to the moor. If he looked up all he saw was the circle of grey sky enclosed by the coronet of the tower.

In the valley below men were running silently, sure-footed as deer, the light touching their helmets and white war shields. The chink of their weapons carried to where he lay as they ran into the west and the soft rain came across the valley like a curtain.

It was all dreams. He had given his life to dreams and now he was dying.

A boy was standing over him; a boy with fair hair.

Allan Condent smiled up at him, 'I was dreaming ... here, help me up.'

Allan drew his coat closer about his shoulders and stirred the embers of a fire that smouldered before him. 'I have not seen you since you left me here.' He shivered and his dark eyes glittered. Yet he whistled the scrap of a tune as he put more wood on the fire. 'I am stronger.'

'You must leave at once,' burst out Finn, white faced with anxiety. 'Soldiers, about twenty of them. They came marching up the hill to the Castle. Cissie and I watched them come. I did not dream it was for you but it is. Someone told us and we came straightaway.'

Allan held his hands to the crackling yellow flames throughtfully. For the first time he seemed to see the dark, girlish head in the background.

'Cissie. How many others did you bring?'

'Only Barney. Don't worry, he's a donkey, Cissie's donkey. He's tethered outside.'

'Did Dermot send you?'

'No. We saw the soldiers when we were in the High Street. They were marching up the steep to the Castle in their red uniforms. A man came behind me and whispered. He said, "Tell your friend in yon tower they come for him," then he was gone.'

'I will not eat you, Cissie,' said Allan. 'Come nearer. What did this helpful gentleman look like?'

'Like a fox,' said Cissie, bursting into speech. 'Red hair. Stink like a fox, too.'

'Drink, I think,' added Finn.

Allan watched the flames. 'It does not sound like anyone I know. Where would you take me?'

'I heard Dermot talking last night. He said he had sent a message to your friend in Porlock asking him to be ready to take you off in case ...' Finn's voice trailed away. He looked miserable.

'In case?'

'In case Lady Condent could not be trusted,' muttered the boy.

'Soldiers at the Castle. I think Dermot's judgement does him credit. You are children,' he said, after regarding the flames for some moments more, 'I am dangerous company. You had better leave me here.'

'I would die first,' said Finn; his voice seemed to choke him, so fierce was the feeling in his breast. 'I will not let you be taken. I will not. You have done nothing wrong. Cissie knows – '

'Cissie?' Allan turned to her.

'Finn has always stood my friend,' replied the girl simply.

Allan waited but she seemed to think she had said enough. He looked at her more carefully. 'I would I had found such a companion when I was your age.' He said to Finn, 'Help me stand up.'

It was accomplished with difficulty. His knees buckled; but by supporting his weight against the wall and leaning on Finn, he managed to stand, after a fashion.

'The French say . . .' he panted, 'the French say it is the first step which is the worst.' He staggered forward two or three steps and halted. 'They lie.' He was like a man at the end of a race. 'Now for the noble Barney.'

It took long enough to get him astride. There was no saddle and the only place he could hold was Barney's sparse grey mane.

'We brought him straight from the field on the way up,' said Finn miserably. 'I daren't go back to the mill for a horse because of the soldiers.'

'Barney is fine with me.' Allan's voice was light, but he was slumped forward, his face grey with pain. He looked ragged and muddy; a scarecrow figure whose feet trailed the ground. It was as well their path took them over the loneliest part of the moor. They made a ludicrous spectacle.

Finn decided to stay at Allan's side for fear he fell off, leaving Cissie to lead.

'Come along Barney, come along do, there's a dear,' said Cissie beseechingly. Barney was browsing among the low shrubs of whortles and heather; his head had to be wrenched away before he could be jolted into motion. Although he was cast in the uncomplaining mould of the rest of his tribe there was about him an unnerving streak of independence. As well as his tendency to stop and eat whenever he saw a tempting mouthful, Cissie warned them not to let him linger too long about the black puddles which dotted their path. 'He do like to wallow in 'em, see?'

Finn tore a switch from a bush; every pause on Barney's part was rewarded by a cut on the rump.

Allan did not complain; spasms of pain chased across his face as the iron bones of the donkey drove through him with every step. His complexion as grey as dead ashes. Despite this, his features twisted with amusement at the figure they cut.

'The bold Fenian,' he observed. 'Pulled by a girl and pushed by a boy. Hard to tell which is the donkey.'

'Will you use your gun should the soldiers come up with us?' asked Finn.

'Flight is my only hope,' was the reply. 'This is my last throw.'

As they climbed and gained the ridge, the sea, flat and grey, came to lie placidly all along beneath them. On the other side the valley merged into the hazy blue of the woods. Great brown tracts of heather spread out before them as far as they could see, and nothing stood between them and the sky. They made their snail's progress; Barney did not seem able to proceed at anything more than a slow walking pace. Allan relapsed into silence and part-unconsciousness. Finn kept glancing behind, though he saw nothing but a flock of gulls whirling like white scraps above the valley.

'What did you come out into the wilderness to see?' said Allan suddenly, gritting his teeth at the pain in his belly.

'Lord bless us,' said Cissie, in alarm.

'He is wandering a little, I think,' said Finn.

Allan was swaying so much they had to stop for Finn to steady him.

'Finn, dear,' said Cissie. 'This riding don't do him any good, you know.'

'If they catch him they will hang him; even though he is innocent of any wrong,' said Finn coldly. 'You don't have to be here. You can go home if you wish. I would ask you only to leave Barney. I will return him safe to you later.'

'That an't just, nor fair,' replied Cissie. 'I come because you and your friend are in trouble. But he is as about as sick as any living man can get.'

'They will hang him,' repeated Finn. 'I – we – can save him.'

'Is he so dear to you?'

'Yes.'

Allan seemed to come to himself at this; he turned his head and regarded Finn seriously, but did not speak.

Put all the time they had been together and it did not amount to much more than a week. Yet Finn knew the feeling he had for the Fenian.

'Come on – ' he said, violently yanking at Barney's head. 'We must get on.'

They plodded on.

He is the bravest man I know, thought Finn miserably, I love him.

'What was that!' he cried, looking back.

116

'Naught,' said Cissie. 'You are anxious and becoming addled. I thought you had a cool head on your shoulders, Finn Hagan.'

'I thought I saw something glint in the distance.'

'Do you remember that first night at the mill?' Allan said, between breaths. 'When you were asleep you looked so like your mother I wanted to reach out and touch you.'

'What's he saying now?' demanded Cissie.

'It's nothing.' Finn was embarrassed. As for Cissie, she was becoming jealous and beginning to feel excluded. Perhaps she should have gone home.

'I knew Finn's mother when she was a girl,' Allan said gently. 'I was even more foolish then than I am now. She would have married me but I would not give up the Brotherhood I had newly joined. She married Dermot instead.'

'You poor man,' said Cissie. 'Did it break your heart?'

Allan coughed. 'Not then,' he said. 'Only now.'

Finn looked at him with new eyes. Oddly, the thought of Allan married to his mother did not seem so strange. Her manner towards him, distant yet at the same time quick and responsive argued a special feeling. Then there came a surge of loyalty to Dermot. Strong Dermot, who always knew what to do; who always looked after them.

'Dermot was the better man,' said Allan, as if reading his thoughts. He gasped as Barney stumbled in a hole. 'What will we do when we reach Porlock?'

One hand strayed towards the wound in his stomach.

'I have thought of that.' Finn was glad to leave the other thoughts behind; to store them up for later. 'We will hide you in a wood until dark. One of us will stay with you while the other goes into town to find the man with the boat and tell him you are waiting. After dark we will bring you in and get you away.'

Allan kept his hand over the place in his stomach. His eyes were closed.

'Oh my Lord,' said Cissie. 'You did see something. Look.'

Over the ridge, about a mile away, they came. They could see them plainly; the red jackets, white bandoliers; buckles and badges catching the light. Calm and steady they came, two abreast; marching with a purposeful tread that was remorseless.

117

'There's someone ahead too,' said Finn, urgently, 'looking at us.'

Cissie jerked her head back. 'Barty Purvis,' she said in disgust. 'Talk about a bad penny. If he tells the soldiers, we're done for.'

'Allan has a gun.'

She turned to him in horror.

'To make him come with us,' said Finn. 'I could make him come with us.'

The troop of soldiers, twinkling away in the distance, were vanishing down a dip in the track. Barty had not even seen them.

'It don't need a gun to deal with Barty Purvis,' said Cissie. 'You keep a hold of your Allan and leave me to do the talking. Barty don't like you.'

Barty waited, still as a post, two rabbits dangling at his waist.

'Fancy seeing you, Barty,' said Cissie sweetly. 'Can't talk. Once Barney stops it's the very mischief to get him going again and we must get help for this poor gentleman.'

Barty's wide blue eyes were fixed in astonishment on the mud-spattered figure slumped upon the donkey's back. 'What's going on?'

'We are taking him to the hospital in Porlock,' said Cissie, keeping them moving. 'He's very poorly.'

Barty fell into step with them. He eyed Finn, then turned his gaze back to Allan. 'He looks like he bin sleeping rough for a week. There an't no hospital in Porlock. Only that big house where they lock up all they loonies.'

'How very sharp you are, Barty,' said Cissie, with a glance at Finn. 'He's a runaway lunatic. We're taking him back.'

'Is he now?' said Barty, withdrawing a little. 'I never seed one afore. Make him say summat.'

'He isn't an animal to do tricks for you,' burst out Finn hotly.

'There now,' said Cissie, smoothing this over at once. 'Truth is, Barty, we have bitten off more than we can chew. It needs more than two of us. It needs one to lead, one to hold the poor lunatic in place, and another to give Barney the odd switch across the backside. Two of us can't do it, see? Do come and help us.'

'Not I,' said Barty, stopping dead. 'I be afeard of mad things.'

118

They moved away, leaving Barty standing on the track behind them.

'Shame on you,' observed Cissie. 'We bin paid good money for this job.'

'Wait,' Barty ran and caught up with them once more. 'How much money?'

'We–ll,' Cissie considered. 'We could let you have a shilling as your share.'

Barty stopped and thought the terms over. He ran up once more. 'Give us sixpence now and sixpence when we get to Porlock.'

'We haven't got the money in sixpences,' said Finn. They hadn't a brass farthing between them but they could worry about Barty's payment when they got to Porlock. The main thing was to keep him away from the soldiers. That they were on their way to Porlock too, he did not doubt. It was where the moorland road took them. It would be a logical thing to do. 'You'll have to wait 'till we get to the town.'

'You wouldn't rogue me?' demanded Barty, looking at Finn suspiciously.

'We wouldn't ask you if we didn't need you. I never knew we were such good friends.'

'Ah well, that's true enough,' said Barty and struck Barney a terrific blow. 'May as well begin to earn my shilling.'

The donkey plunged, Allan's mouth opened in a silent gasp of pain. Finn clutched at him until Barney settled once more.

'Another leap like that,' whispered Allan, 'and I am a dead man.'

'What did he say?' demanded Barty eagerly. 'What did the lunatic say?'

'He said,' Cissie replied furiously, 'that you are even a bigger fool than you look. What are you trying to do, kill him?'

Barty hung back.

'Oh come along,' she said with contempt. 'You are a poor thing, don't dawdle.'

Even if they allowed Barney no respite their progress was still lamentably slow. For Finn the thought of marching feet gobbling the distance between them was a torture.

'How come,' Barty stumbled along behind, still smarting from Cissie's tongue, 'how come you two have gotten care of a lunatic?'

'We found him,' replied Cissie tersely.

Finn looked with horror at Allan. The wound had opened again; there was a dull stain seeping into his waistcoat.

'Then who's a going to pay us?' persisted Barty.

'I will,' said Finn. 'One more word out of you and you will be paid more than you bargained for.'

Barty stared back at Finn but said nothing; contenting himself with a defiant sniff.

They had been climbing all this while and had now reached a plateau of dry heather spotted here and there with stunted and twisted trees. The wind moved it all like a dull brown sea. Their road, no more than a cart track, lay before them for miles. Porlock was still a long way off.

'Not so far now,' whispered Finn.

Allan's chin was on his chest, he seemed not to hear.

'Please stay awake.' He started, finding Barty at his elbow. Barty was gaping at Allan.

'Mother!' cried Barty pointing. 'Oh, I wish I had never come. Take him down, take him down.'

He had seen the blood. Drops of it had fallen on to Barney's back, some on to the track.

'How cold his hands are,' said Finn hopelessly. 'He had better rest. Barty is right.'

The three of them helped him down and laid him as gently as they could among the springy heather. As he was put down the flap of Allan's coat fell open to reveal the butt of his revolver sticking up from his belt.

Barty sprang away from them as if stung. 'I'm going.'

It was heavy and needed two hands to steady it, but Finn dragged it free and pointed it at Barty.

'You're going nowhere.' There was a determined edge to his voice. 'Sit down.'

'Mother!' Barty crumpled abruptly beneath the shelter of a gorse bush. 'He an't a lunatic and there an't no sixpences. Don't point that thing at me, Finnie. I won't go.'

120

Cissie was rubbing Allan's hands between her own. 'He's stone cold. Finn, what are we going to do?'

'We aren't going to do anything,' said Finn. 'I want you and Barty to go now. I'm sorry for pointing the gun at you, Barty. This isn't your affair, nor yours, Cissie. If you leave now the soldiers won't know you were with me.'

He knelt beside Allan. Cissie stood up and Barty came over next to her. They stayed watching.

Allan Condent was slipping away. His troubled heart was easy. Though Cissie said truly, his hands were cold, he felt warm and alive. He could hear feet, many feet and they were running, the chink of arms, the clatter of a shield. He wanted to be with them, running into the west. But there was something he had to say first –

'I thought I could hear marching!' cried Barty. 'Look, soldiers!' He was pointing back down the track. 'Get down!'

They threw themselves among the heather and lay still. They were less than a rifle shot away; the soldiers coming towards them in one solid marching body.

The red and white of their uniforms blurred and ran together like watery paint, as Finn watched through eyes that were slowly filling with tears.

'Go on – ' he whispered. 'Before they see you . . .'

'They've stopped,' Cissie said, ignoring him. 'See, one of 'em's found something on the ground.'

The men had drawn up in their twos and halted. One of them was examining the track; he appeared to be kneeling, he touched the ground and then walked back to the rest of the company.

'Blood,' observed Barty. 'He must of bin bleeding afore we noticed.' Oddly, since the appearance of the soldiers his sympathies had shifted towards Finn; as if he naturally took the opposite side to the forces of law. 'We never had a chance, Finnie.'

'Go now,' insisted Finn. 'We can't do any more.' He stood up and moved back, his arms helplessly by his side, the long revolver against his leg. Cissie came and touched his hand, 'Come with us, Finn.'

Finn shook his head and turned to Allan Condent but a further movement among the soldiers had attracted Barty's attention. 'Come and watch!'

The soldiers had unslung their carbines and were now carrying them at the ready. They had spread out into two equal groups on either side of the track like beaters on a pheasant shoot.

'Make her go with you, Barty,' said Finn quietly.

Cissie took one last look at Finn and allowed herself to be led away by Barty.

'Sorry, mister,' said Barty, as he passed the prone figure of Allan. 'I never meant thee no harm when I made thik donkey jump.'

If Allan heard he made no indication. Finn went back and stood over him, looking down.

The Fenian's dark hair moved in the wind; Finn found himself remembering that first night when he had been reading some tale of adventure and escape with the wind booming in the chimney. It seemed an age away.

He knelt down. Allan's hand moved and found his arm.

'There is something I have to tell you,' he whispered. His breathing was rapid and shallow, 'I tried to stop it . . . you believe me, don't you?'

Finn nodded. A tear splashed on to Allan's upturned face.

'My life . . .' he paused and gathered breath. 'All wrong . . . all wrong.'

'No,' Finn shook his head fiercely. 'No. Mother says you are brave and kind.'

'Bless her for that . . . but it was all folly.'

There was a longer pause. A small bird perched among the heather began to chirp with a harsh sound, like two stones scraping together.

'There is something I have to tell you . . . kiss me, Finn.'

As he bent to the cold face, wet with his own tears, Finn felt a sigh touch his cheek. There was no struggle. The bird chirped as the last breath of Allan Condent was gathered up into the wind that swept through the heather on its way to the sea. Whatever it was Allan had wanted to tell Finn was unsaid.

The small bird swooped away to another perch. What had

been Allan Condent lay perfectly still; his curly hair stirred in the wind; his hand fell gently away from its place on Finn's arm.

Finn lifted his eyes heavenward; a sky, immense and blank, was all there was.

Deliberately the boy bent and planted a kiss on the cold cheek. The wind ran through the heather, touching it everywhere with the marks of many light feet; as if a great army of running men were making their way to the west.

Finn walked back to where he could see the soldiers. Among his grief a knot of something dark and implacable was rising to his throat, strangling his breath.

Masked as he was by the gorse, they did not observe him. They plodded ever closer, honest brick-faced Saxons who would stolidly drive a man to his death without question. They were no more than eighty yards away now.

Without aiming, he cocked the hammer of the Colt and fired it.

The line of red coats disappeared into the heather. Even as the crash of the revolver echoed around the hills, sharp orders were shouted and a score of rifle bolts rattled.

There followed an uneasy pause. He had stopped their advance. Finn remained where he was.

'Allan Condent!' came a cry. 'Throw down your weapon and come out with your hands raised. There are too many for you to fight. Come out and we will not harm you!'

If only he could, thought Finn, looking back to where the Fenian lay.

'Allan! Allan, d'ye hear me? 'Tis Dermot!' The figure of Dermot Hagan stepped out boldly on to the track, cupping his hands. 'The officer says he will hold his fire if you will send the children down!'

Here and there the black helmet of a trooper reared above the line of heather and was gone.

'Let them come down, Allan!'

Finn jumped. Cissie was standing by him, Barty a few yards off.

'We came back,' she said. 'We got to thinking how we shouldn't leave you.'

123

She slipped a hand through his arm. 'He's dead now,' she said quietly. 'All his pain is finished now.'

Finn looked down at her, dimly wondering how a girl like her could know such things.

She started to move and he came too. 'Let us walk down the path. Your father is waiting. The soldiers won't hurt us.'

Later, when the officer had finished with his questions and Allan Condent had been secured across Barney's back, Finn stood with Dermot and watched the party make its way back down the hill.

'Father,' he said, his voice bitter and empty of tears. 'What will happen now?'

'Father?' Dermot nodded to the jolting tarpaulin covered figure that was being taken away on a donkey. 'I'm not your father. That's your father.'

CHAPTER SEVENTEEN
The Witness

To have lost a father before he owned you; to have known him before in a different relationship; there came to Finn the numb sense that the world had shifted.

'Dermot is not my father?'

His mother laid aside her knitting; left off rocking the new cradle with her foot; she held him though he kept his arms by his side. His eye was bright and feverish, his cheek flushed.

'If love means anything, and time, and looking after. Then he is more your father than he is of that baby there.'

'No,' said Finn. 'He is so proud of her, his little Mary Elizabeth.' He let his hand droop over the cot and the baby seized it, clasping one of his fingers with all her hand. He gazed into her eyes and felt only a great puzzlement. A man dies; a baby is born. One door closes, another opens.

'It is so hard . . .' he hesitated. He continued to look away from his mother, studying his half-sister with a frown. 'Why did you not marry Allan?'

She drew his other hand to her so that it touched her cheek. Neither did she look at him but at the small face nestling in the cot. 'I would not,' she said slowly. 'I refused him. He was . . .' she cast about for the best words '. . . A fighting man. Though he gave up the army he could not settle. He wanted revolution – ' She gripped his hand more tightly. 'He could give nothing up for me. He wanted to marry and fight his battles at the same time. I told him to break my heart at once. I could not give it to him so that he might break it piece by piece. Can you understand that, Finn?'

He shook his head. How jagged their lives were; they left him bleeding.

'I lived through the Hunger,' continued his mother urgently, looking up at him now. 'Was I wrong or selfish because I did not want my life tainted by hatred? Well, I refused him, right or wrong, though he had got me with child and I was shamed. Little I cared . . .' She touched his hair '. . . I called you Finn after all those stories he so loved. Dermot, who was our friend, offered to take me to England. Not to marry me, but out of respect, to save me further shame. Allan went away to America. Dermot looked after me as if he was my husband and after you as if he was your father. I came to love him for it, to want to marry him. I have never regretted that. Not for a moment.'

'Who am I?' whispered Finn.

'The son of a great man.' Dermot had come in from the mill and his voice rang around the kitchen. 'Not some old miller who never struck a decent blow in his country's cause.'

'I was happy as the miller's son,' said Finn.

Dermot approached, his eye bright. 'My poor Finn.'

They embraced and Finn buried his face in the miller's broad and dusty shoulder, feeling his strong arms all around him.

'Did he love me?' His own thin shoulders were beginning to shake, 'I think he did.'

'Ah, sure . . .'

'And can I still stay here with you?' His face was glistening.

Dermot laughed, a deep gentle laugh, and folded the boy in his arms again. 'And where else would you be staying?'

His eyes caught those of his wife, 'We shall put him to bed and give him a warm drink, Mary. These past few days have been too much for him.'

There had been no action taken against any of them. The officer had visited Lady Condent and told her gently that this had been decided out of respect for her position; that and the fact that her son had been guiltless in the incident which had wounded him mortally. Even had he been caught he would have been charged with complicity but no one believed he would have been found guilty in view of his efforts to prevent the explosion.

She was grief-stricken; but even among the dark mists through which now she walked, she knew there were some decisions she must take. She sent a brief note to Tipson. She was in need of advice and Pinecoffin, by now, was repugnant to her. It was he, she suspected, who had informed against her son.

She followed Allan to his last resting place alone. She stood in the small graveyard which served the Condents and allowed profuse tears to wet her wintry cheeks. There should, in justice, have been others there but she did not want them. She wanted to take this moment alone. There would be time for justice later.

On the appointed day Tipson limped up to the castle and spent some time with her. It was drawing on to evening when he emerged, leaning on his stick, thinking thoughts of his own warm fireside. It was not to be. Halfway down the drive he was surprised by a figure coming out at him from behind the shrubbery.

'Schoolteacher? Just the man. Glenlivet.' A blunt hand with dirty nails was proffered. 'Been lying in wait for a witness. Thought you'd never come out. Prosy lady.'

Tipson smiled his crooked smile. 'I do not think we have met, Mr Glenlivet.'

'That we have not,' agreed the other. 'But you have been mentioned as a gentleman who knows what's what. Oblige me, sir, by stepping this way and being my witness. Very important.' He winked mysteriously.

Tipson, being a man who was charmed by anything out of the way, agreed readily enough and Glenlivet led the way through the shrubbery with many whispered injunctions to silence and caution.

Pinecoffin, meanwhile, was chafing in the most uncomfortable place. He was skulking in the Chinese pagoda which during the milder months served as a summer house. At the moment it was draughty enough to give anyone an earache; it seemed to have trapped the east wind, which whistled this way and that, trying to get out again.

'Glenlivet . . .' said Pinecoffin bitterly, in the utmost misery, wrapping himself in his own short armed embrace. 'Where is the villain? Confound him. Goes to all the trouble of naming this ridiculous spot and then doesn't bother to turn up. I've a good mind to go in – '

His toothache was playing him up; he was longing for a drink.

127

But he daren't leave. Truth was, he was terrified of Glenlivet; a violent man who would choke you to death soon as look at you and laugh while he did it. He knew too much. It was the cursed drink and laudanum which had made him blab that afternoon and he had regretted it bitterly ever since. Life was getting uncomfortable. Lady Condent had withdrawn the sun of her countenance; things had become decidedly chilly –

'How de do. You dog.'

Pinecoffin jumped. 'Oh it's you.'

'Ye dinna sound very pleased to see me.' The disembodied face of Glenlivet presented itself, leering, at the open window.

'I'm not pleased,' replied Pinecoffin peevishly. 'Try sitting in here for two hours. Have you any idea how cold it is? What is it you wanted to say?'

'Just this.' Glenlivet made no attempt to come in. 'The game's up.'

Pinecoffin stared at him, 'The game's up? Is that why I've been dragged into this unspeakable wilderness of a garden and kept cooling my heels for hours? Heels did I say – ha, you should have my bum. It's got no more feeling in it than an ironing board. Of course I know the game's up!'

'It's the boy,' said Glenlivet, with a wicked grin. 'Damned fly in the ointment if I ever saw one. D'ye realise he's her grandson? When the old lady snuffs it he'll get the lot. It means you murdered Vellew for nothing.'

'Will you keep your voice down!' cried Pinecoffin, restraining an impulse to grab his confederate by the throat. 'I did not murder Vellew! We quarrelled and he slipped into the river. It was a fortunate accident, no more. Now will you please to come indoors where I can see all of you. You give me the horrors grinning away like that.'

'Naw,' said Glenlivet. 'Out here I can see if anyone creeps up on us.'

'How in Heaven's name did you come to pick such a spot as this?'

'I canna come to the house too often. D'ye think the old lady has willed all her fortune to your Cause? I mean, if she was to die now, all would not be lost?'

128

Pinecoffin stammered. He felt colder than ever. 'What do you mean?'

Glenlivet made his eyes bulge and drew a finger across his throat.

'She's an old lady,' faltered Pinecoffin.

'Or the boy. I'll take him bird nesting and push him off a cliff. Then we'll be back to just the old woman, since your feelings are so tender in that direction. You can carry on milking her for every penny she's got. How much have you had so far?'

'A lot,' admitted Pinecoffin miserably. 'I don't know where it all went. Thousands we had – Sammle and me – perhaps there isn't that much left. Let's not bother, hey?'

'You are a milksop!' sneered Glenlivet.

'I rather think I have heard enough,' said a third voice.

Pinecoffin thrust his startled head out of the window. The schoolteacher was limping into view from behind the shelter of one of the pagoda's walls.

'There is no need to torment the wretch further.'

Pinecoffin swallowed. There was something almost cruel in the way Tipson looked at him.

With a theatrical flourish, Glenlivet who had half turned away, removed part of his nose. From being squat and indeterminate of shape it had become long and rather fine. 'I'll keep the wig on as it keeps my head warm. The sidewhiskers are glued on or I'd whip them off too just to add to the effect.' His yellow tooth glinted.

Pinecoffin felt as though he was being smothered; he pointed a faltering hand, 'You're – '

'George Dando,' said that person, with a bow. 'My nose being gone, I am – to paraphrase the Bard – man again.'

'You said you were dead! Or rather *he* said you were dead. Oh Lord!' Pinecoffin clapped a hand to his brow and pinched his cheek hard with the other.

'I nearly was,' said Dando. 'The story about the alley was true. I crawled away on my hands and knees. Most heroic.'

Pinecoffin continued to stare.

'No, this ain't one of your dreams. No more golden city for you, my lad.'

'But why?'

'Because I felt like it, that's why. I didn't know Allan Condent was in that tower when I come to see you. I was after whatever money was going, that's all. But when I learned that such a worm as you had put that gentleman's life in jeopardy I decided to do you.'

'Well you've done me,' snarled Pinecoffin. 'Shopped me good and proper.'

'There is matter here for the gravest concern,' interposed Tipson. 'Evidence of fraud and worse. I imagine if we make enquiries we will establish you are not even a clergyman.'

'I never said I was,' said Pinecoffin, recovering himself a little. 'You can't nail me on that one. I had a mission among the harlots of Wapping – we would read a little together and pray . . . wish I'd stayed with 'em. Wish I was there now. They may have been poor but they were honest.' He directed a meaningful glance at Dando.

'While you are neither,' said Tipson calmly. 'May I suggest that your day is over? Lady Condent desires to be rid of you – she confided as much to me this afternoon. She is in no fit state to withstand any further shocks. Revelations about her Cause and Vellew's death had better be postponed. I will keep what I have heard to myself for twenty-four hours. That ought to give you ample time to leave. You may make your departure in peace and quiet – no one will pursue you. As long as you do not return I will tell no one of what I have heard – in the foreseeable future.'

Pinecoffin slunk away.

When he had gone they sat down together on the bench he had lately vacated and watched the dark filling the valley.

'There is one thing that is not clear,' said Tipson at length. 'And that is your own part in all this.'

Dando stood up and leant on the window-sill. 'He was a fool,' he said angrily. 'All his life.'

'Pinecoffin?' Then following Dando's gaze to where the tower showed dimly over the trees, 'Oh, I see . . . you knew him well?'

'We were soldiers together.' Dando swung round, as if he expected to see Tipson smile. He did not. 'Does it surprise you that I have been a soldier?'

'Not in the least.'

'I was an actor and then I was a soldier. Now I am a spy – both my previous professions preparing me for my present one. Though honesty – a virtue I am not given to – compels me to admit I was a poor hand at both. Pinecoffin was right – this place is the very devil. Shall we walk?'

They took the opposite direction, away from the castle, along the side of the hill which overlooked the mill. It was dark now, though they could hear the mill wheel turning, somebody whistling as he crossed the yard to shut the gate.

'I found myself a volunteer – by whatever means I forget now – in the 10th Ohio regiment during the American War. Allan Condent was my commanding officer – there were a lot of Irishmen with me, all swearing oaths to some secret brotherhood or other. I confess I was very interested – you never know when knowledge of that nature will come in useful. Indeed, I have been living off it for some time now. The whole regiment was a hotbed of Fenianism. I was wounded . . . in the thigh.' Dando fixed the schoolteacher with a fierce look. 'The upper thigh . . .' he growled. 'The backside you might call it.'

'Tell me about it,' said Tipson, without a flicker.

'We were surprised by the enemy somewhere in Virginia. I was eating some filthy concoction, the usual dog's mess they served up as dinner – I wasn't even wearing a shirt or boots – when suddenly the man sitting next to me pitched face forward into the fire. I started to drag him out – I didn't realise he had been shot until I was hit myself. I thought I was dead. It's funny – I took a bullet in that ignoble place and thought it had killed me. I remember looking at the sky and thinking how beautiful it looked. But not sad, perfectly happy, ready to go to wherever it is dead people go, while all around bullets slapped into the mud or flew over my head. Our men had found cover in a small copse and were returning fire. I noticed all this as if I was watching from somewhere else. It was nothing to do with me. I felt perfectly tranquil. I was happy – ' Dando stopped and grasped his companion's arm, 'that's it. It was the happiest moment of my life. And then . . .'

'And then?'

131

'And then my arse began to throb and I knew that I had been robbed of the dignity of an honourable wound. Furthermore, Allan Condent, with his usual disregard for his own personal safety – and I hated him for that, why couldn't he be a coward like me? – was crawling on his belly over twenty yards of exposed ground to drag me to safety. There wasn't one of those yards I didn't curse him.'

'You owed him your life, I think,' put in Tipson.

'He was so stupid! He believed in bravery and nonsense like that – it was he who was the play actor, with his head stuffed full of those ridiculous Irish stories of his. Those games they all played with their passwords, their boasts of how they would free Ireland from the tyrant's yoke. I hated them all.'

'And you turned informer.' Tipson could not keep the coldness from his tone.

'Gladly. It has proved a useful source of income.'

They had come to a gate.

'My horse is stabled at the Condent Arms. I suppose the boy, Finn, will now inherit?'

Tipson nodded, 'Though Lady Condent will not see him. She says the pain of it will be too much to bear. She has asked me to make arrangements for his education – '

'Well,' Dando looked at him. 'You will shake my hand?'

'Gladly.' They clasped hands. 'But why did you warn everybody of the soldier's coming? Why did you expose Pinecoffin?'

'He was a little man. I am a little man. Allan Condent was not. I owed him and his son that much. Good night, schoolteacher.'

Tipson watched him walk away. In his mind's eye he could see Dando swept away on life's tide, always bobbing about in the unsavoury backwaters where all the rubbish, the discarded, the flotsam and jetsam collected.

And yet, he thought with a sudden flash of insight, and yet you loved him.

CHAPTER EIGHTEEN
Fire

Back to the old game. Back to Wapping, old cock.

'Don't want to go,' replied Pinecoffin tearfully, hugging his glass and staring into a bare fireplace.

Not before time, continued the voice in his head, been here too long. Think of it! Think of the Ratcliffe Highway, gals with red stockings and tight little bonnets, nodding their heads and grinning in the gaslight. Don't it make you all fluttery to think of 'em? Oh Lord, all that sin they wallow in.

'Oh Lord,' echoed Pinecoffin, aloud. He could see a city, all its domes and roofs and turrets, its walls and windows, all of it bathed in a warm golden glow. He ached to be able to go in. The eternal city, the heavenly Jerusalem, his own golden city where there was warmth and languor and repose. But he was locked outside with the voice of a hoary old sinner pouring his poison in his ear. Saying things, dirty things.

''T'idn't fair,' he whimpered and took another drink. As the alcohol and the soft drug it contained warmed him, his city dissolved into a shimmering sea where the sunlight burst into a thousand diamonds.

Drunk as a pig, said the voice in disgust. You can't stay here now. It's all over. We've had our whack, it was good but it went on too long. We was bound to get caught. Let's get out while we can.

He was in Vellew's old office. He had begun to think of it as his own but now it was dark and cold. There was no fire and ringing brought no servant to attend to him. Perhaps Lady Condent had told them to ignore him. More likely they chose not to hear; he had never been popular with them and now the old lady had locked herself away, they could do more or less as they chose.

133

He picked up the lamp and walked over to the window. If he held up the lamp to the window all he saw was himself holding a lamp. Without the lamp there was nothing and that was worse. There he was, a forlorn figure in black, like a mourner at a funeral. He settled his necktie and brushed his suit with his fingers. It was crumpled where he had been sitting over long, but somehow he couldn't get really interested in his appearance. As if he wasn't really here.

Course you're here, growled the voice in his head, fool.

Pinecoffin was fingering the curtains, picking out the pattern of the heavy brocade; leaves and petals and unlikely looking fleshy flowers, all twined themselves together in such a way he couldn't see where one started and the other left off. It made his head swim.

'They're all against me,' he said bitterly. 'Even you ... yes Sammle, even you.'

Stop talking to yourself, said the voice roughly, go and pack.

He dropped the lamp. It was as if he had lost interest in his hand. It fell with a smash near to where the curtain touched the rug. A thin blue flame ran playfully along the rug and the curtain began to smoulder. Pinecoffin watched, fascinated.

Put it out, commanded the voice of Samuel Wentworth, put it out. Ring for help.

Pinecoffin cleared his throat, like a man about to make a weighty pronouncement. 'Shan't.'

It was too late, even if he had wanted to. Orange flame blossomed, brightened and warmed the room, casting a golden glow over his sickly countenance. Then it leapt, like a wild tiger, half-way up the draperies in one bound.

Pinecoffin backed away, upsetting his chair, the room was as bright as a thousand suns. The cold white walls had been transformed; they were glowing.

'The golden city!' he whispered.

It was so bright, and oh, so warm. He was inside it now. It was stupendous.

Earlier the same evening Finn was walking with Dermot. It was the first time he had been out since his illness. He had the feeling, which sometimes comes after a fever, of ease; as if now he could see things with clarity, as they really were.

'Tell me again what Mr Tipson told you when I was ill.'

'Only, well, she seems to have appointed him as her agent. She has locked herself up to be alone with her grief.' Dermot glanced down at the boy. 'She took it hard – your grandmother – as if, he said, she was regretting what her life had been up to that point and it was too late to change. She must have loved him in her way. Hard to understand. Particularly as she doesn't want to see anyone.'

'But she spoke about me.'

'Wants to send you to school. A gentleman's school.' Dermot's heart was heavy. 'Wants it all done properly. One day you will be master of all this.'

He waved his hand at the castle and its surrounding countryside.

'Yes,' said Finn. '*He* wanted that too.'

Since Allan's death Dermot and Finn had been uneasy, yet at the same time yearning for each other. Everything was changed; but Finn wanted him to know that they were the same to each other as they always had been. He had lain three days thinking, his thoughts burning and painful.

'It's what we all want, Finn.' Dermot kicked at a stone in his path. Their walk had passed in silence until the boy had mentioned Tipson.

'It was easier before,' said Finn.

Dermot studied him. He was paler than usual, his fair hair had grown long, brushing his collar. Nothing but the determined set of his mouth marked him as his father's son. He was growing into a fine boy.

'It was easier when you were my father.'

'But I'm not.'

'Mother said you were and she's right. You looked after me, loved me.'

'I love you,' agreed Dermot quietly.

'And he is my father too. And *she* is my grandmother.' It was getting cold, he slipped his hands up his sleeves the way his father used to. 'I have been thinking there is a madness in the Condents.'

Dermot laughed. 'Allan was not mad.'

'Look at her – saying he was dead all this time and then becoming half-dead with grief herself when he does die. Look at him, giving up his family, his home, his confederates, to die on a hill watched by three children and a donkey.' Finn spoke angrily, with a pent-up violence.

'He was a great man.'

'Look at the man who built the tower!' went on Finn, ignoring him. 'He was a Condent too!' They had been there, with no word spoken, and looked at the ashes of a cold fire. 'An empty tower that can be seen for miles. Empty. What good is it? Yet every day hundreds of people lift their heads to look at it.'

Dermot watched him through narrowed eyes.

'I thought my brain would burst thinking of it all.' Finn's head was bent, a frown of concentration on his brow. 'What good was his life . . . was it a madness?'

'People will lift their heads to look at it,' said Dermot.

Finn put a hand on his arm. 'I think so. I wish I could be sure.'

'And what about Finn? Finn Hagan that was, Finn Condent that is?'

'I don't know. I will do my best,' said Finn slowly. 'For you and my mother. For Cissie. Even for the old lady in the castle.'

They looked towards it and stopped in horror. There, on the opposite height, Condent Castle was blazing like a beacon.

CHAPTER NINETEEN

The Promise

The flames loomed against the night sky, cracking like whips, dancing and ducking, licking their tongues through every window in the east wing. The roof was caving in, timber by timber, sending up a swirling pillar of sparks with every collapse. By the time they reached Castle Hill, gasping for breath, half the building was in flames.

To Finn there was something devilish in the way the flames cavorted through the roof; as if they were met at some fiendish celebration. The house, in its last agony, groaned in pain when each timber fell spilling its tiles, spewing red sparks in an upward spiral. Allan Condent had wandered through this house in his childhood, dreaming of Finn Mac Cool, gazing through its windows, his imagination making Ireland out of the Somerset landscape. Now this house was dying. The same windows were bursting and exploding with the heat.

It was bright as day on the grass where the watchers stood. The crowd was growing by the minute as more and more grim-faced villagers hurried up the hill. It was like some grotesque Fifth of November, a bonfire seen twenty miles away, watched in silence by the awestruck inhabitants of Monkton. An attempt was made to make a human chain of buckets from the well but, as one link in the chain observed, you might as well spit at the fire for all the effect they were having. The usual number of people bustled about self-importantly, but as the fire engine had been sent for there was nothing for them to do; and even their directions were issued in a respectful whisper.

Finn watched with a sharp pain in his chest. He wanted to howl like a dead man's dog. The house was dying; soon there would be no link with his father left at all. Above the main door the arms of the Condent family were blackening before his eyes as streams of smoke from the empty windows billowed across them.

'No sign of the Missus,' said a voice near by.

'You mean Lady Condent, neighbour?' enquired Dermot, his beard and hair like spun silver in the fire glow.

'Her and that Pinecoffin chap are still in there. All of us is here, else.'

So even his grandmother was dead. He had wanted to do something with the new life his father had wanted for him, but it seemed fate was determined against that. The pain as he watched surprised him with its intensity.

Now the central part of the house was beginning to be devoured. Tiles exploded with short sharp reports, like gunfire; thin licks of flame flickered here and there along the roof. Thick black smoke, and then thicker, was pouring from the windows.

'There! Look at the windows!'

The cry was taken up and the watchers lifted their eyes, shielding their faces from the glare and heat with their hands.

A figure stood alone, among all the smoke. She studied the watchers below with an indifference which chilled every heart. Despite the intense heat, and with the same air of studied calm, she stepped back out of sight. There were waving hands, cries of supplication, shouts of advice, but of the figure there was no further sign.

'Someone ought to do something!'

But what? And who? Some men ran forward clutching a covering snatched from a waggon. They held it beneath the window and called up but the heat beat them back. They returned once more only to have fragments of blazing wood rain down on them from the eaves of the roof.

It was his grandmother; no one else's. Finn gazed up at the second floor window and felt his heart swell, as if he had taken a deep breath. She was Allan Condent's mother.

And taking that breath he ran forward towards the house where the heat was so intense it was solid; a palpable barrier which he had to push through, his eyebrows shrivelling, his skin drying and cracking almost at once.

He ran with his head down and his eyes all but shut. There

138

were shouts behind him but he could not hear what they were saying. He ran at a tangent, taking a line which led him close to the blaze and then further away. There was a small door, like a postern, some distance from the main door in a part of the house which was not burning as badly as the rest.

The well of the doorway was cooler as he rested his cracked face against the stone, and sobbed for breath. The handle on the door was a black iron ring. It turned easily enough; he had time to see a stone spiral staircase ascending into the gloom above before stepping in and closing the door behind himself.

It was peaceful in the dark. The noise of the fire had been shut off and there was no heat, though smoke swirled in eddies through the darkness and made him cough. He went up slowly, flattening himself against the wall, keeping low where the air was breathable. Something ran over his feet and skittered down the steps. A rat, he supposed.

Lady Condent had appeared at a second-floor window. When he did come to a door in the wall he ran his hands along it but did not open it. It was hot to the touch; the smoke was much thicker here and he could hear the fire sizzling and popping on the other side. He continued upward. though the smoke, now pouring in from the door below, reduced his progress to a coughing and choking crawl on hands and knees. His eyes were streaming; he kept them closed, relying on touch to tell him where he was.

It was a relief to come to a second door; another well-oiled ring which let him out into a passage. He recognised it at once from the day he had tea with Lady Condent.

The air was still filled with blue and red from the great stained glass window on the stairs but there was a more sinister, brighter light, playing behind it; it served to colour the smoke which billowed here, as everywhere, to illumine the portraits of his ancestors, who gazed sombrely down at him, as if they knew this was the end and doubted his ability to do anything about it.

Lady Condent was standing in the entrance of a large room with her back to him. She was watching its destruction with a curiously polite and uninterested air; as if it was an entertainment

139

got up on her behalf which she didn't greatly care for, like the mummers' play at Christmas. She did not move.

Finn went up and touched her arm. She turned at once and gazed at him with eyes that were dull and lifeless. He had not seen her since that day of the tea and was struck at the difference in her. Gone was the sharp, abrupt manner. She looked like an old lady, shabby and lost in her old shawl and down-at-heel shoes.

'You must go at once,' she mumbled. 'All the other people are gone.'

Finn kept hold of her arm.

'You mustn't stay here,' he said. 'There is no time to be lost. The roof will fall in.'

He spoke slowly, with great patience, as one would to a child.

'Your face,' she remarked. 'Your poor face.'

'I came for you. To bring you out,' Finn led her back along the landing where the smoke was blue and red and thicker than ever. 'I am Finn. Allan's son.'

'Finn,' she said wonderingly. 'Your face is burnt.' His skin was blistered, his hair singed.

'This is the way I came in,' he said calmly.

But the stairwell was filled with a smoke so dense it drove them back coughing for air. They could not go down that way; and the staircase below that stained glass window was in flames. The fire was now in the room Lady Condent had just vacated, devouring the hangings, blackening the plaster, running along the floorboards; the furniture was ablaze, chairs and tables crackling like logs.

Finn faced about; he could think of nothing to do.

'Is there any other way?'

'So,' she said sadly. 'You came into a burning house to die with me.'

'I did not. I have come to bring you out, you are my father's mother – my grandmother.' As he was speaking Finn dragged her by the wrist away from the fire, down the passage, trying each door as he came to it. All the rooms seemed to be bedrooms. 'Neither of us will die,' he panted. 'My father is dead before I knew him. I will not let you die. Think, is there no other way?'

She looked bewildered along the passage.

'Think,' he said urgently. 'No one knows this house as well as you.'

'There is ...' she looked down the passage once more. 'At least I think there may ... it is such a long time ago.'

At the very bottom of the passage stood a tall grandfather clock. It ticked steadily in the face of impending doom and would, no doubt, go on telling the hour until its very hands melted.

Lady Condent reached the clock and opened the door that disclosed its workings with fumbling hands. She studied its painted face.

'Made in York. It was this one, I'm certain ... it was such a long time ago.' She groped about with her fingers. 'I'm sure this is the clock. Yes,' she caught her breath, 'here is the catch ... but it is stiff, so very stiff.' She looked more like the lady Finn remembered; she had lost her bewildered look. 'Or perhaps my fingers have stiffened with age also. We used to play here when we were children.'

There was at last a click. 'There is a key also. Ah, here it is.'

She drew it out.

'The clock is fastened to the wall so that no one can move it. I have released the catch which holds it there. Now, together we must shift it to one side.'

It was done without great effort. Behind the clock was a narrow wooden partition with a keyhole. Lady Condent inserted the key and the door swung inwards.

'It is a stone staircase which leads to the cellar. Similar to the one which brought you up to me but much smaller. The steps are very narrow. You must lead me down.'

She gave him her cold fingers. Finn entered the gloom warily; the stairwell was free of smoke and the air, though dank, was blessedly cool on his face.

Lady Condent giggled. The effect was so startling Finn almost stumbled.

'I have not been here since I was a child. We were allowed to play here on rainy days. I do not think it has been used since. The man who built this house loved secrets and secret passages.

I believe this one was built to help recusant priests escape capture – not that I know it was ever used.' She laughed again; her laughter, oddly fresh and girlish in the dark, echoed around the old stones. 'What fun we had in those days.'

Finn was feeling the wall with one hand, guiding her with the other, 'Did you show it to Allan when he was little?'

She allowed herself to be led down three more steps before answering and when she spoke the laughter had withered. 'No.'

'He would have liked it, I think.'

'How is it,' she said wonderingly, 'that you know what I, his mother, did not?'

In the dark the question was easily asked, though not so easily answered.

'We forget,' she went on, 'if we are too serious we can forget our own childhood. He asked me why I did not love him when I had the chance. I have been a vain and selfish old woman.'

The darkness was palpable, unrelieved by any shaft of light. Down they went. They made slow work of it and as they descended both minds were on the one who linked them; whose presence in the gloom was all around.

'You were with him when he died. Did he say anything about me?'

There was an awkward pause. Finn was desperately trying to frame some comforting lie.

'Do not lie to spare my feelings.'

'No'm.'

'You cannot know what a reproach that is to me,' she sniffed abruptly. If she was crying he couldn't see.

'Who was the girl who was with you?' her voice came muffled and sudden. 'They say you are sweet on each other.'

It was the turn of the darkness to hide Finn's face. 'Cissie Creech,' he said loudly, too loudly, as he blushed. 'One day I will marry her.'

'You sound very sure. I have never heard of such folly – a Condent marry a village girl!'

'He was not afraid of folly,' retorted Finn. 'I knew him long enough to learn that much – not to be afraid of doing what you think is right.'

She made no direct answer. Her fingers curled around his; they were warm now and soft, gently he drew his thumb across them in an involuntary caress.

'After all, what will you have?' she muttered. 'A burnt out shell of a house, an estate bled dry by a leech, a foolish old woman for a grandmother. Marry whom you please, Finn. Pay no heed to me.'

They had come to the bottom. All the way down the air had been clear with only a whiff of smoke here and there. 'Good stone,' said Lady Condent approvingly. 'Good solid stone. Here is the door and now we are in the cellars.'

It was somewhat lighter in the cellars and Lady Condent, who seemed to know exactly where she was, found a lantern hanging on a nail and after a small struggle, lit it.

The door of the secret staircase had swung to behind them; two small barrels indistinguishable from the rows of barrels all about them.

'And another door,' said Lady Condent, shifting a barrel opposite to reveal a wooden partition like the one upstairs. 'We must hurry, people will be worrying about you, perhaps risking their lives.'

It was the passage to the Folly which she had so lately trod with Pinecoffin. They made their journey with as much speed as they could muster.

'I will do my best for you,' said Lady Condent. 'I promise I will.'

These were things best said in the darkness and she said it not with her usual firmness but in a voice that often trembled.

'He wanted us to know each other,' replied Finn. 'That is what all this has been about.'

Lady Condent sighed; a sigh of sudden, unexpected happiness.

It took them less than an hour to get to the tower and back to the castle. The memory of it was a blur to Finn; walking all that way hand in hand, pausing wordlessly near the spot where Allan had lain, the roar of mingled surprise, joy and relief at their reappearance outside the smouldering castle; the hand shakes, jostling, back slapping and white faces mooning and crowding into his

143

vision. Of all the faces there was one that called to him; the small, pale, tear-streaked face of Cissie.

He did what he had never done before; putting out one rough arm, he bent his head and kissed her.